Mct

An Emma Harrison Mystery
Book 2

Wendy Cartmell

Costa Press

Copyright © Wendy Cartmell 2015
Published by Costa Press
ISBN-13: 978-1514286739
ISBN-10: 1514286734

Wendy Cartmell has asserted her right under the Copyright Designs and Patents Act 1998 to be identified as the author of this work.

All characters and events in this publication, other than those in the public domain, are fictitious and any resemblance to real persons, living or dead is purely coincidental

This is a work of fiction and not meant to represent faithfully military, or police, policies and procedures. All and any mistakes in this regard are my own.

Inspired by a friend and fellow writer.

Praise for Wendy Cartmell

'A pretty extraordinary talent' –
Best Selling Crime Thrillers

'This is genre fiction at its best, suspense that rivets and a mystery that keeps you guessing.' –
A R Symmonds on Goodreads.

Also by Wendy Cartmell

Sgt Major Crane books:

Steps to Heaven
40 Days 40 Nights
Honour Bound
Cordon of Lies
Regenerate
Hijack
Glass Cutter

Emma Harrison Mysteries

Past Judgement
Mortal Judgement

Author Note

Her Majesty's Young Offenders Institute (HMYOI) in Reading is no longer a working institute. However, the building is still there and plans are being considered by Reading Council to turn it into a hotel and leisure complex.

The prison has a long and rich history and its most notable prisoner was Oscar Wilde, who wrote the Ballad of Reading Goal, based on his incarceration there.

I worked as a teacher in the Education Department at Reading HMYOI, teaching a range of subjects including English, Maths, Computer Skills, Art and, rather badly, Cookery. I loved my time at Reading and also at other nearby prisons, where I did supply teaching. My family has experience in prison education. My father was Deputy Chief Education Officer for Prisons and Borstals in England and Wales in the 1970's and 1980's and my mother taught at Reading Prison and Broadmoor. Both had the dubious pleasure of meeting some of Britain's most notorious prisoners.

Whilst the Judgment series may draw on our experiences from time to time, all characters and events are fictitious. Although I try and be true to policies and procedures, this is a work of fiction. Therefore, all mistakes are my own.

One

The Whisperer had just received a telephone call. A sly smile spread across his toady face as he replaced the receiver. He resisted the urge to rub his hands together in glee. Just. He looked at his watch. It was only 2pm, so he had plenty of time to get ready for the night shift.

He walked up the wooden stairs, which were still wearing the floral wool carpet he'd put down in the 1970's, and went into the spare bedroom. He pulled out his prison officer's uniform from the hulking mahogany wardrobe in the corner of the room. Sniffing a sleeve, he decided it smelled a bit musty. Then putting his nose in his armpit, he decided he smelled a bit musty as well. To kill two birds with one stone, he'd hang his uniform up in the bathroom while he had a shower. That way the steam would freshen the fabric and make the creases fall out. He put his hand in the wardrobe again and pulled out a white shirt. Turning it around on the hanger, he decided that it needed an iron. He'd do that after his shower.

Collecting the uniform, he walked into the bathroom and hung it up on the corner of the shower stall, leaning inside to turn on the water. Slipping off his dressing-gown, he caught sight of his middle-aged paunch in the bathroom mirror. He knew he really should do something about that. Partake in some kind of exercise. Maybe join a gym? But he wasn't really a gym kind of person. Anyway, his nightly activities took up most of his time. He practiced his art at night and then gloated over it during the day. He shrugged his shoulders. He wasn't one to worry about his appearance for the wart-like pustules that covered his face and neck had put paid to any illusions he'd had that someone might find him even remotely attractive. But that was okay, he'd come to terms with his disfigurement. And anyway, his whisperings were far more enticing than any woman could possibly be. The doctor hadn't been able to help, when he'd asked him about the warts on his face. He'd just said they were probably the result of stress. Well, he could appreciate that, he supposed. The last year had brought him more stress than he could ever have imagined. Since Janey had gone...

He climbed into the shower and washed his short dark hair. He'd grown it long at one point, thinking the hair might hide some of his blemishes, but it hadn't really made any difference, so he'd cut it again. Anyway he needed it to be short for work. He washed his face, feeling the coarse hair of his bushy eyebrows between his fingers and his fat lips under his palms.

As he soaped himself he could feel his excitement growing. Tonight was going to be special. He could feel it. It had been a week or so since his last visit to HMYOI Reading, a young offenders institute and he was eager to see how effective his whisperings from last week had been.

Two

The cell walls closed in. Sometimes Jimmy even fancied he saw them move, out of the corner of his eye. He looked around the cell. It contained his stuff, but no people. He'd stuck up on the wall photos of those he loved, yet had pushed away. Photos of those he'd lost, through his greed and temper. And look where it had got him - incarcerated in Reading Young Offenders Institute: in other words, in prison. Gone was the car, the money and the drugs, to be replaced by a solitary existence. He was no longer the 'big man' on the outside, just 'scum' on the inside.

How stupid he'd been in his ignorance and how quickly his arrogance had turned into despair. Now all he had to look forward to was the prospect of long days, long nights and even longer years spent behind the high walls of whatever prison the authorities deemed fit for him. Where were his mates? His fellow gang members? They were gone, all gone. Still out on the town, living their lives, with no thought for him at all.

Jimmy pushed his hand through his dark hair. It was greasy and needed a wash, but he just couldn't be bothered. Couldn't even remember when he'd last had a shower. But then he didn't have any reason to make himself look presentable. There had been a change of clothing available that morning and he hadn't bothered with that either. He'd just stayed in his cell. After all he was on basic regime, confined to his cell 23 hours a day, so what difference did an hour make?

He sat up from where he was lying on the bottom bunk and looked at his hands. They were full of scabs from where he'd hurt himself. He'd stabbed them with anything he could get his hands on. His neck was full of scratch marks from where he'd run his nails down his skin time and time again. Hurting himself in order to feel the pain, which offered some small release. It was the only thing left to him. The only thing he could control. Every other aspect of his life was organised by others. He was in their hands and they weren't kind hands. He knew that. He'd heard the whispers at his door.

"Serves you right, being in prison is all you're good for."

"You need teaching a lesson."

"Drug dealers are the scum of the earth."

"You're a good for nothing. You'll never make it on the outside. You'll just go back to your gang and then end up in prison again. What sort of existence is that?"

Maybe the whispers were right. Maybe he wasn't good for anything. Not any longer. He'd no purpose, no mates, no reason for living.

His mum had visited him earlier that day. Jimmy had seen the pain in her eyes, seen how much he'd hurt her. She'd tried to bring him up the right way, but somewhere along the line he'd taken a different path. What he'd thought was a more exciting path. He'd turned his back on his mum, her life, her faith. The look in her eyes was worse than anything the courts, the prison, the police had done to him. That visit had been a defining moment. He now knew what he had to do.

Running through his brain, over and over again, were words that he'd heard in church when he was a small boy.

'Yeah though I walk through the valley of the shadow of death

I shall fear no evil.'

Psalm 23. That was it. That was what he was doing now - walking through the valley of the shadow of death.

He'd learned the Psalm when he was still his mum's good little boy. The little boy she was proud of, loved and looked after. But he'd shunned her. He'd thought that the praise and adoration of his mates transcended a mother's love. How wrong he'd been.

He stood, pulled the sheet off his bed and began twisting it with his hands. Repeating those words from the Psalm as he did so. As he wound the sheet round and round, so he shouted the words over and over again, "Yeah though I walk through the valley of the shadow of death, I shall fear no evil."

Someone nearby called out, but he took no notice. He couldn't hear their words, lost as he was in his mantra.

Three

Sonya Hill was worried, very worried. That afternoon she'd made the journey from London to Reading, to see her son in Reading Young Offenders Institute and couldn't believe what she'd seen. Her confident boy had shuffled into the visiting room, head down, so his face was hidden by dirty, greasy hair. He appeared to have lost weight, his prison issue clothes hanging loosely on his once muscular frame. Where had his swagger gone? She'd always secretly loved it. Even though his confidence came from being a member of that awful gang, it had turned him into a handsome young man, someone who walked the walk and talked the talk. So it was such a shock to see the change in him.

He'd sat down at the table and looked at his hands, not at her. She'd tried to talk to him, but he'd seemed miles away. Lost in whatever agony had him in its thrall. He hadn't seemed to know she was there at all.

She'd strained to hear what he was mumbling. Maybe it was some sort of rap? A song he'd heard and loved during one of the many open mic nights he was so keen on going to and organising. He was really into hip hop music and she had hoped that it would help him through his incarceration.

Leaning over the table as far as she could, without alerting a prison officer, she'd struggled to make sense of what he was saying. It seemed religious. Then it had dawned on her. Her son was reciting the Lord's Prayer. Where the hell had that come from? It had been years since he'd been to church. Years since he'd rejected her religion for his own brand of faith – a faith that was his gang, his mates, his music, his drugs.

"Jimmy? Jimmy, are you alright?" She'd put into those few words all the love she felt for him, hoping her emotion could cut through the miasma of despair that swirled around her son like a protective force field.

He'd raised his head. For a moment the confusion in his eyes had cleared and she'd felt he'd seen her, known who she was. A single tear ran down his cheek. He hadn't bothered to wipe it away. He'd just dropped his gaze and started mumbling once more.

Sonya hadn't had a moment's peace since the visit. She was trying to work out what to do. She should phone the prison. Her hand reached for the telephone. She touched it, then retrieved her hand as though her fingers had been burnt. No, they wouldn't take any notice of her, so she decided to have a cigarette instead. With shaking fingers, she'd tried to get one out, dropping the packet in the process and scattering cigarettes across the tiled floor. Picking one up, she managed to light it and sat at the kitchen table smoking and thinking.

What would the consequences be if she did nothing? She paced the small kitchen, her slippers slapping on the floor. Could she live with herself if her son got worse? Didn't get the help he clearly needed? She shivered as though cold and wrapped the dressing gown more tightly around her slight body. Her hand reached for her mobile phone once again. This time she picked it up and called Reading Prison.

A leaflet she'd read about self harm and depression in prison, had said something about being able to talk to The Safer Custody Team, whoever they were, so when her call was answered she said, "Could I be put through to the Safer Custody Team, please? I want to talk to them about my son, Jimmy Hill."

"Sorry, no one from the team is available."

"Not available?"

"No. They work office hours and as its 10pm, there's no one there."

The man on the other end of the phone didn't seem pleased to hear from her, nor very willing to help.

"So who can I speak to?" she asked.

"Must it be tonight?"

"Yes, of course, it must be tonight."

Sonya was trembling. She wasn't the most confident of people and was easily deflected. She had the character of a mouse, not a lion. But she wasn't going to be fobbed off. Not this time. She had to make someone take some notice of her.

"It's my son, Jimmy Hill. I'm worried about him."

"Mrs Hill, I'm sure most mothers of the lads in here, are worried about their sons. That isn't a good enough reason to talk to someone about him, especially at this time of night."

"Look, he's not well, I'm telling you. I saw him this afternoon, he's depressed and he needs help."

"Well, depression isn't uncommon."

"For God's sake," Sonya tried not to shout. "He's hurting himself. I saw the marks and the scabs. He's losing control, mumbling and talking to himself. I've never seen him like that before. I'm frightened. Desperate. Please, you've got to help him."

"Very well, Mrs Hill, I'll put you through to the Duty Manager." The officer could be heard clicking a couple of buttons and sighing rather dramatically. But Sonya didn't care. She was determined to get Jimmy some help.

"Duty Manager," a rather tired female voice answered the phone.

"Oh, thank goodness," Sonya gabbled, hoping that a woman would be more compassionate than the rather dismissive man she'd just spoken to. "I'm ringing about my son, Jimmy Hill," and she went on to explain what had happened earlier in the day.

"I'll see what I can do, Mrs Hill. I'll make a note of your concerns and pass them on."

"Pass them on? Who to?"

"To someone on the wing."

"Thank you. Please, get someone to make sure he's alright. Get the officers on the wing to go and check on him, something, anything." She knew she sounded desperate, but couldn't help it.

"I'm sure he'll be fine, Mrs Hill. Try not to worry," and before Sonya could get the name of the person she had been speaking to, the phone went dead.

Sonya phoned the prison at 11pm but was told there was no news. She phoned at midnight, after drinking a glass of wine for courage and again was told not to worry. It was 1am when her phone rang. It was someone from the prison to tell her that her son had been found dead in his cell. It seemed he had committed suicide. They were very sorry for her loss.

Sonya's scream echoed up and down the lonely halls of the block of flats, where she now lived on her own.

Four

Emma Harrison entered Reading Young Offenders Institute through the main gate, showed her ID and got her keys. Just the normal start to a normal day, until the officer booking her in said, "Heard the news?"

"What news?" Emma wasn't really listening to him, as she tried to clip her keys onto her key chain.

"Oh, you haven't been told then."

"Told what?" Emma managed to force the reluctant clip onto the chain and looked up. "For God's sake, Clive, stop pissing about. What news?"

It was too early for riddles and Emma wished Clive would stop being irritating and just get on with it. She'd had a nightmare journey into work, the Reading rush hour traffic had been bumper to bumper, all the way down the A329 and she had a headache threatening over one eye.

"It's young Jimmy Hill. He was found dead in his cell in the middle of the night."

That was not what Emma had imagined he was going to say. It hadn't even been on the radar. She'd thought he would just be imparting some juicy bit of gossip, not the terrible news of a death. Emma had to hold onto the security booth as she processed the shocking information.

"Dear God, no," she whispered, her brain not wanting to accept the truth of Clive's statement. "You mean my Jimmy Hill? Are you sure?"

"He's the only one we have by that name that I'm aware of," Clive replied, turning back to his logs, putting his initials by her signature, as though the death of a young inmate meant nothing to him. But that wasn't the case for Emma.

"Shit! I've got to get to my office," she said and hurried down the corridor towards the Administration offices.

She burst through the door, handbag slung over her shoulder, files she had been reading over last night in preparation for today, in her arms. She was struggling to get out of her coat. Her auburn waves bounced on her shoulders and her eyes were wide with shock behind her tortoiseshell framed glasses.

Joan, the administration secretary, looked up from her desk at Emma's arrival and said, "Ah, Emma, glad it's you. The Governor wants to see you."

"And I want to bloody well see him as well," Emma snapped. Then stopping at Joan's desk she said, "Sorry, I didn't mean to be rude." Pausing for breath, she then added, "I'll just dump this lot and then go and see him. I guess it's about Jimmy Hill."

Joan nodded, turned her chair around and looked at her computer, but Emma caught the tears in Joan's eyes. Joan had been at Reading HMYOI for many years and Emma knew Joan had a strong mothering instinct. The demise of any inmate would no doubt hit her hard, the long years she'd been at the Institute seemingly not diminishing her commitment to the boys in their care.

Emma, herself, wasn't so much sad as angry, very angry. Jimmy Hill was one of her lads. Being Assistant Governor for Inmate Welfare, she'd become very concerned about him over the last few days. He'd been segregated after becoming violent and was on basic regime and Emma had expressed her fears for his mental state if he had continued in segregation. But no one else had agreed with her at the time. And now look what had happened. But the thought that she had been right, gave her no satisfaction at all, just a deep sense of responsibility and sadness.

Using the time it took to walk from her own office to the Governor's she took deep breaths, forcing herself to relax and rolled her neck to try and take the tension out of her upper body.

Knocking on the door, she heard, "Come in," and Emma walked through the door into Governor Sharp's office, her small heeled shoes not making any sound as she walked across the carpet to his desk.

"You wanted to see me, sir?"

The Governor was looking dapper as usual. His suit was more Massimo Dutti than Burtons and she was sure the new tie he was wearing was silk. He was going prematurely gray as he was only in his early 40's, but that only seemed to add gravitas to the overall impression of a man completely in control of both his prison and himself.

"Ah, Emma, yes, thank you. It's about," the Governor paused and looked at a file on his desk, "ah yes, Jimmy Hill," he read out loud. He looked up from the file. "Oh, from the look of you, you've already heard the news."

"Yes, Governor, I've been told he's dead, but that's all I know at the moment. What happened?"

"Sit, down, please," and after she complied, settling into the seat and crossing her trouser clad legs, he continued. "He was found hanging in his cell last night. Officers did what they could, but there was no chance of resuscitating him."

"How long?"

"How long what?" The Governor peered at her over his reading glasses.

"How long had he been dead before they found him?"

"Yes, well," the Governor coughed behind his fist, "that's something I intend to find out. There's a meeting at 2pm in the conference room. We'll go through everything then," and he began to fiddle with a pen on his desk.

"And that's it?" Emma realised she was expected to leave.

"Sorry?"

"That's all you have to say? He's dead. Full stop. End of story."

"I beg your pardon?" Sharp's previously sombre expression hardened and he glared at her. "Emma, may I remind you that you are an Assistant Governor in this establishment and as such you are expected to behave like one. So I suggest you put Hill's death into perspective and get on with your job. It is all very unfortunate, but we still have a prison full of inmates to run. Do I make myself clear?"

Emma stared back defiantly. But then realised she had to capitulate. At least for now.

"Yes, Governor," she replied, dropping her gaze.

"Very well, I'll see you at 2pm. Please bring all the information you have on Jimmy Hill with you."

When the Governor bent his head to his files,

dismissing her, Emma stood up and left the office, cursing Sharp, Chief Prison Officer Robinson and anyone else she could think of, but this time cursing them in her mind not through her mouth. However, if Sharp thought that was the end of her protests, he was dead wrong. She'd have another go in the meeting later that day.

Five

Everyone was in the conference room by the time she arrived just as her watch said 2pm. Governor Sharp was at the head of the table. Chief Robinson, looking confident with every inch of his military bearing on display, was on the Governor's right hand side. Chad Albright, Head of Operations was on his left. Emma didn't want to sit next to either man, but chose Chad as he was the least obnoxious. He was far more timid than Chief Robinson and although he was dressed in a suit and tie, he managed to look scruffy when compared with the Chief's immaculate uniform.

"Now Emma has arrived, perhaps you could start, Chief," said the Governor making Emma feel as though she were late, which of course she wasn't. It appeared the three men had arrived early. Had they had a meeting before this meeting without her? Oh well, she figured she'd soon find out.

"Could you start with how Hill had been prior to the unfortunate incident please?" the Governor asked the Chief.

Sharp had arranged his features into something vaguely resembling sadness, but his tone was more one of irritation than compassion. It meant Emma was unable to shake the feeling that the Governor considered the incident was more unfortunate for the prison, than for the boy and his family.

"Very well, Governor," Robinson said. "Jimmy Hill had been exhibiting problem behaviour for the past few days. He'd become violent, had altercations during exercise and had been talking to himself."

"What had he been saying?" asked Emma.

"Mumbling some sort of religious stuff according to the officers on duty at the time."

"Not normal behaviour, then?"

"No, Miss Harrison." The Chief always refused to call her by her first name. Emma was sure he did it to wind her up. "Not within the realms of norm even for this place."

"Please carry on with your report, Chief," the Governor glowered at Emma for daring to interrupt.

"Due to his erratic behaviour it was felt that he should be segregated for his own good."

"His own good?" Emma spluttered, pushing her hair behind her ears as though better to hear the Chief.

"Yes," said Chief Robinson emphatically.

"Don't you mean for the good of your officers? For I can't see how putting a troubled young man on basic regime, in what is effectively solitary confinement, would have been good for him."

"We did that after discussions with Mr Albright."

"But not after discussions with me."

"No."

"Nor Geoff Fox? Please tell me you consulted the Medical Officer?" Emma pushed her glasses up her nose.

"At that stage we felt it was more an operational

matter than a welfare matter, or a medical one."

"Clearly," Emma glared at Chief Robinson. "Did you go and see Jimmy?" she asked Albright.

"Miss Harrison, I think I'm the one that should be asking the questions," the Governor rebuked her.

"Sorry, Governor," Emma apologised, but carried on with her question anyway. "Did you?" she looked at Chad.

"What?" Albright looked frightened to death. His eyebrows lifted in his bland face and his lips formed a perfect 'o'.

"Go and see him?"

"Yes, of course," Albright managed to recover some of his composure and said, "And the Chief was right. Jimmy's demeanour was very odd. He wasn't his normal self at all."

"But you didn't see fit to put him on suicide watch." A statement rather than a question, for Emma already knew the answer.

"To me, he was exhibiting signs of having taken drugs and was having a bad trip. That was all."

"That was all! Dear God! But you've experience of suicide protocol, wasn't that what you did in your previous posting? What on earth made you think his problem was drug related?"

"I, um," Albright thumbed through his papers, looking down at them instead of up at Emma. "I can't actually recall why at the moment, but I know there's been a problem with drugs getting into the prison. A number of the lads have been turned away from Education for being high on various substances."

"I think that with hindsight, perhaps Mr Albright would have dealt with this young man differently. Wouldn't you agree?" Sharp looked at Chad.

"Yes, sir, I would agree with that sentiment."

Chad Albright threw the Governor a look of gratitude and reminded Emma of a drowning man hauled from the water by his saviour.

"Good, then that's settled."

The three men closed their files. Emma thought she was hallucinating. Were the three stooges really closing the case and insisting on pretending that they hadn't done anything wrong?

"Is that it, sir?"

"For the moment, Emma, I believe so."

"But the investigation?"

"Will be carried out by Chad, as Head of Operations, of course."

"Well, in that case, perhaps the Head of Operations would like to interview me? Now?"

"All in good time, now if you'll excuse me."

As the Governor stood, the other two men followed his lead and Emma was left sitting at an empty conference table. No nearer to understanding what had caused Jimmy Hill to behave as he had and with very little confidence that she would ever find out.

Six

Governor Sharp barked at Joan as he passed her desk, "Get me Geoff Fox. Now."

Sharp walked into his office, around his desk and sat down in his luxurious leather office chair, glad to be out of the meeting. He ran his hand through his normally obliging hair, which had, since the meeting, decided to flop over his forehead. A sure sign that he was rattled. Pushing it back into place he reflected that it was all that stupid girl's fault. Emma Harrison. He really shouldn't let her get to him. An inexperienced assistant governor causing trouble was not in his career plan, which had been honed to perfection and was already reaping the expected rewards. He had a faultless record at Reading HMYOI and was looking forward to securing a post in a larger establishment within a couple of years.

A tap on his door roused him from his musings.

"Come!" he shouted and Geoff Fox materialised around the door.

"You wanted to see me, Governor?"

"Yes, come in and sit down. It's about this lad who committed suicide."

"I'm afraid I wasn't informed of the young man's troubles."

Fox seemed quick to jump in and cover his arse. As expected. There was a lot of that going on today. The thought caused Sharp to sigh in exasperation.

"I know, Geoff," he said looking at his Medical Officer, suitably dressed as a doctor, complete with white coat, biros in his pocket and stethoscope around his neck. "But there's going to be an inquiry into his death. Questions will be asked and I need to know if you are going to be able to answer those questions."

"Well," Fox squirmed in the visitor's chair, set to one side of Sharp's desk. "I can only do my best with what limited resources I have."

"And are you?"

"What?" Fox looked startled, as though he were a deer caught in the headlights of a car.

"Doing your best with what limited resources you have?"

"I believe so, Governor. But, you see, if only you would raise the embargo on recruitment, then I could employ another nurse, which would make all our lives easier."

Fox fiddled with his tie, which seemed to be some sort of thin, blue affair. Sharp idly wondered if it was part of the current fashion, to go with Fox's shirt, which was of a dark blue pattern with a plain white collar. He himself preferred timeless elegance. Mrs Sharp had often told him he looked like a consultant from Harley Street. A description he was immensely proud of.

"I think you're missing the point, Geoff," Sharpe said.

"Am I?"

"Yes. The point is that your job is to maximise your resources, limited or not. Hone your procedures, cut down waiting times, keep a better eye on your budget."

"I'm trying, Governor." Fox now looked like a rabbit, rubbing his wobbling nostrils with the back of his hand. "It's not easy," he mumbled.

"I'll tell you what's not easy, Geoff," Sharp leaned over his desk. "Not easy is working in the National Health Service in an overcrowded, understaffed hospital. Where you are expected to see an inordinate number of patients, every day, from the never ending river of human suffering that is the Accident and Emergency Department."

Sharp saw Geoff could no longer meet his gaze and his eyes had dropped to look at a stain on his trousers, which he was ineffectively picking at.

The Governor pushed home his point. "So, isn't working here looking after 290 odd inmates better? Even if, God forbid, they were all ill at the same time you'd still be better off here than at the local A&E! Let's face it most of the time all you have to do is to dole out Paracetamol or stitch a flesh wound." Sharp laughed at his own wit, but saw Fox looked terrified rather than humoured. "Do you take my point, Geoff?"

"Yes, Governor, but if you'd just come down one morning and see the queue waiting to see either myself or the nurse, perhaps you'd understand better?" Fox finished his little speech, with a red flush creeping up his face and neck.

"Geoff," Sharp leaned back in his chair. "I don't need to come down to see you one morning. I am well aware of how your clinic works. You seem to be losing sight of the solution. You are the solution, Geoff. It's down to you to make it work. I've given you a nurse, a fully stocked clinic and even a hospital wing. I don't see what else I can do to help. Believe me, Geoff," Sharp lowered his voice, "I will not allow this prison to fail. If it does, it will be because of staff letting me down. Not the other way around. Now, the way I see it, your choice is clear. Go away and do your job properly, or start looking at the situations vacant. Which is it to be? Are you with me, Geoff? Or against me?"

"I'm with you," mumbled Fox.

"Thank you."

Sharp sighed with satisfaction and got rid of the miserable excuse for a doctor, sending him scurrying back to where he belonged.

Seven

Emma sat outside Reading Coroner's Court, her insides feeling as though she were on a roller-coaster ride. She would soon be called in to give evidence at Jimmy Hill's Inquest and she wasn't looking forward to it at all, being very much afraid that Reading HMYOI's reputation was about to be sullied. She stood and starting wandering along the corridor, smoothing down her best business suit as she sauntered. It had been a designer label knocked-down bargain from the outlet shopping centre in Portsmouth and normally made her feel elegant and professional. But today the old magic wasn't working. She'd read and re-read the establishment's report into Jimmy's death, until she was word perfect. Everything would be fine, as long as the barrister stuck to the script.

She hadn't expected to be called to the Inquest at all. She thought it would just be Chief Robinson and Chad Albright, but some bright spark thought that as Jimmy was under her remit of inmate welfare, she could have something to contribute. As if. She might have been able to prevent his suicide if someone had called her. But no one had and she would have to live with that for the rest of her career.

"Calling Emma Harrison," an usher appeared at the door to the courtroom.

She followed him in, feeling like Daniel entering the lion's den. In her nervousness she kept winding a lock of hair around her finger. Once she had taken the oath, she answered the question from the barrister, which was to clarify her position within Reading HMYOI and her duties.

After that straight forward question, the barrister, Johanna Blackstone said, "Miss Harrison, at the start of these proceedings, the Coroner told the jury that they should consider if the prison authorities took 'reasonable steps' to prevent Mr Hill from taking his own life. So I would like to explore the steps taken with you. Did you see him in the days leading up to his death?"

"No I didn't. I hadn't seen Jimmy for a week."

"A week? Why was that?"

"Because I have so many young men to look after, I have to see them in rotation, unless anyone in the prison sees one of them behaving differently, outside the norm and flags it up."

"Anyone? Who do you mean by anyone?"

"Let me see," Emma ticked the list off on her fingers, "Prison officers, teachers, youth workers, solicitors, visitors, anyone at all really."

She looked at her hands, wondering why she'd just done that and clasped them behind her back in an attempt to keep them still.

"And did anyone approach you regarding Jimmy's mental health in the days leading up to his death?"

Joanna Blackstone grabbed either side of her open robe with her hands, looking like a parody of a television barrister. But Emma wasn't in an episode of Judge John Deed, this was real and her replies were being recorded and would be poured over by the jury. She shook the trivial thoughts away and answered Joanna's question.

"No."

"Did anyone approach you regarding the possibility that Jimmy may have been taking drugs leading up to his death?"

"No."

"I see. Did you know that he was in segregation?"

"No I did not."

"Isn't that strange? Aren't there procedures to let you know what is happening to inmates in your care?"

"Yes there are, but I never received the relevant forms."

Emma had anticipated that question and before coming to court had double, triple and quadruple checked her paperwork. If there had been a form issued, she was confident it had never been sent to her.

"How did you find Mr Hill when you last saw him? What was his behaviour like? His demeanour?"

"He was a confident, fit, well behaved young man who was doing his best to get through his sentence and looking forward to the time when he could return home to his mother."

"But those are not the descriptions one would use of Jimmy Hill just before his death."

"No it would appear not."

Emma's hands had gravitated from behind her back as though of their own volition and she was holding onto the wooden lip of the lectern, her knuckles turning white in the process. She forced her hands open and put them by her side.

"What would you have recommended if you had known of his problems?"

Emma paused. The last thing she wanted to do was to drop her colleagues in it, but she had no choice. She had to tell the truth.

"Miss Harrison?" the barrister prompted.

"My recommendation would have been that he be placed on suicide watch. That he not be segregated but sent to the hospital wing."

Emma briefly closed her eyes. She wasn't happy about this line of questioning. She felt she was being led somewhere, like a lamb to the slaughter. There was something coming, but she wasn't sure what.

"Why would you have recommended that course of action?"

"Because my opinion would have been that Jimmy would have needed to be with others who could help him, listen to him and support him. Not left to stew in solitary confinement."

"But that's not what happened?"

"No."

Emma assumed that would be the last of the questions and fully expected to be allowed to leave the witness box. But the barrister continued with her questioning.

"Did you know that Mrs Hill, the deceased's mother, had rung the establishment the night of his death, as she was very anxious for her son's safety?"

So that's what it was. Emma had to hang onto the witness box again, shocked by the revelation, which caused her to sway and feel sick. "No, I did not," she managed to mumble.

"What would you have done if you had been informed, Miss Harrison? And please speak up so the court can hear your responses."

Emma cleared her throat. "I would have told someone to go and check on him immediately and possibly gone to the prison myself."

"But you weren't informed."

"No."

"And Jimmy died."

"Yes."

"Thank you, Miss Harrison. No further questions."

Emma climbed down from the witness box and left the courtroom. She should have been able to walk out of there, head held high, but instead bowed her head in shame for the way Reading HMYOI had treated Jimmy Hill.

Once out in the fresh air, Emma realised she couldn't recall walking out of the courtroom, through the corridors, out of the doors and down the steps. She stopped walking and leaned against the wall of the building for support. That experience had to rank pretty high on the list of low points in her life. She looked at her watch. It was only 11 o'clock, which left plenty of time for the Governor to hear about what had just happened and haul her over the coals. Which he would. With knobs on. She had been completely blindsided by the barrister's questions and had been horrified to hear that the deceased's mother had tried to get the prison to do something about her disturbed son.

Emma had just pushed herself off the wall, ready to walk back to the establishment, when a woman accosted her.

"Pleased with yourself now are you?" the woman shouted in Emma's face. "How did it feel to be torn to shreds by that woman in there?"

Emma looked at her assailant, who was wild with anger and grief. Her beehive hairdo was collapsing and her cheeks were flushed. She was stick thin and looked like a hard gust of wind would blow her over. Her sunken cheeks made her eyes look larger than they actually were and her mouth was twisted into a snarl.

"Mrs Hill," Emma stuttered. But the woman didn't allow her to say anything else.

"You're all the same, the lot of you," she shouted. "No one in that place gave a toss about my son," she gesticulated wildly in the general direction of the Institute.

"Please," Emma tried again, but stopped short when Mrs Hill took a step closer.

The woman's eyes were red rimmed and she had mascara tracking down her cheeks. Her discoloured smoker's teeth were bared. Then she hawked and spat a lump of phlegm, which landed on Emma's cheek.

"That's what I think of the lot of you. You're nothing but cold blooded killers without an ounce of compassion."

Thankfully Mrs Hill then ran out of steam and started sobbing. Emma fumbled in her bag and brought out two tissues, one to wipe the disgusting mess off her cheek and the other for Mrs Hill, who grabbed it and rubbed it into her eyes.

"I don't know about you," Emma said, after she'd cleaned her face. "But I could do with a coffee. What do you say?"

Jimmy's mother nodded her head, blew her nose and allowed Emma to lead her by the arm, away from the Coroner's Court.

Eight

That afternoon, still strung out from the Inquest, Emma decided to seek out the company of the Prison Chaplain, not so much for spiritual guidance, more for moral support. As she walked through the prison, she realised she hadn't really given much thought to the despairing side of working in a prison before. When she'd joined HM Prison Service she had been more concerned with injury to herself from angry or deranged prisoners. Now she was being confronted by inmates who were injuring themselves and worse. And the fact that it was young boys who were so troubled was heartbreaking. Her Majesty's Young Offenders Institute in Reading took those aged from 18 to 21, both those serving a court ordered sentence and those on remand awaiting their day in court. When a prisoner approached his 21st birthday he was required to move onto an adult prison. Not the best course of action for some of them, as she was well aware.

Pulling her thoughts away from Leroy Carter whose move to an adult prison had gone drastically wrong, she knocked on the Chaplain's door.

No reply.

Emma looked at her watch. It was nearly 2pm. Father Colin Batty (who always described himself as batty by name and batty by nature, before anyone could do it for him) was due back from speaking to some of the lads as they made their way to work or education. As she looked up, Batty strode down the corridor towards her.

"Emma, my dear, how are you?" the concern in the Chaplain's voice made Emma blink and swallow. He'd known, of course, that it had been Jimmy Hill's Inquest that morning.

"Um, fine, I think. I just wanted a quick chat, if you've time?"

"Sure, come in and grab a coffee."

Emma followed him into his office, but declined the coffee as she was already wired with caffeine. Sitting in an easy chair in front of Batty's desk, she sighed.

"Was it that bad?" he asked, his well groomed white hair giving him the air of a benign father. His soft voice had a lulling quality to it, which encouraged people to divulge their secrets. He wore his habitual clerical garb of blue shirt with dog collar over dark trousers.

"Worse. But it's not compassion I need this afternoon, which I'm sure you are willing to give," Batty nodded slightly in agreement. "It's rather, how do we go forward from here? How do we stop the suicides happening? How do we support the most vulnerable lads?"

Father Batty leaned back in his chair and crossed his legs. Adopting a casual pose for what was not a casual subject, as they were both well aware.

"You know I can only make recommendations, Emma. If I see an upset prisoner, whatever the reason for his distress, I can only let the wing officers know. I help the prisoners fill out a form with the details of a particular request, say a phone call, a compassionate visit from a family member, whatever it may be. The officers then handle the application. But that's if they get time, if they don't forget, if there's not an incident on the wing, if there are enough officers to cover their duties properly, if there's not a..."

"I get it, Father," Emma stopped him reciting the list of problems. "But how much of these are real problems? Or are the failings due to problem officers?"

Father Batty paused for a moment before speaking. "Be careful, Emma. The last thing you want to do is to make enemies amongst the officers. You know that, you were one of them once."

"Yes, during my training."

"Exactly and some of them resent you graduates you know, with your fast track programme through the ranks."

"Don't I know it, it's not that some of them are rude to my face..."

Father Batty raised his eyebrows.

"Alright, so some are rude to my face, because of their attitude towards graduates like me. Sometimes we're seen as the ones that got away and left them behind. Left them on the wing where they'll stay for the rest of their careers. However, it doesn't mean they're doing a bad job. But you know what they say about a barrel of apples, there's always one bad one. Have you ever come across a particularly resistant officer here?"

"Emma, we all have. I'm not in a position to talk about individual officers and their failings or otherwise. If I do come across anything untoward, then I will raise the issue with Chief Robinson and Chad Albright, or even with the Governor."

"So you just think its overwork, or a mistake, when something gets overlooked."

"That's all I can say at the moment, Emma. I think you've summed it up pretty well. I'm not saying you haven't a point and that you shouldn't investigate. For goodness sake I've sat with upset lads whose mothers or fathers were dying. I've comforted someone sobbing because they couldn't get through to their girlfriend on the phone before lock-down and had to leave things in the middle of a row. It's devastating to the individual. But it's just one component of a very stressful job for a prison officer. And I think that's what we have to take into account."

After a moment, Emma said, "Thanks, Father. I've got to get going, before I drown in anymore paperwork," and she stood up. "But I'm warning you now. I'm going to stay vigilant. The last thing any of us wants is more suicides here in Reading.

"That's a tall order, my dear."

"Don't I know it, Father," Emma said and left his office to get back and deal with her urgent cases. She had lads she couldn't let down. And anyway, if she was going to make waves... The old adage came into Emma's head, 'people in glass houses shouldn't throw stones'. She realised she had to be above reproof herself before accusing anyone of failing to do their job properly.

Nine

Sitting in his empty house, the Whisperer decided to get out his wedding photographs. After making a cup of tea, he retrieved the album from the bottom of the television cabinet and sat on the settee with his cuppa on the low coffee table in front of him. Placing the book on his lap, he carefully turned the pages. The photographs were protected by sheets of tissue paper and he carefully peeled away the first one to look at the photograph beneath.

There she was, his Janey, alive, vital and beautiful. That was the way he wanted to remember her. He didn't want to think of the wasted skeletal figure the cancer had transformed her into. He pushed away the memory of her illness and turned the page. The next photograph showed them surrounded by their friends and family, everyone looking so smart in their finery and so happy for him and Janey. Happy that they'd found each other, that they'd found love in their later years.

The next photograph wiped the smile from his face and soured the remembered happiness. It was a picture of Janey and her good for nothing son, Dominic, from a previous marriage. Dom had been using drugs even then. You could see it in his spaced out eyes, his vacant smile. He was clutching his mother's arm. It looked like he needed to hold onto her to help himself stay upright. At the time he'd only been using recreational drugs, at least that's what he'd told them. But his addiction had escalated. Eventually he had started using heroin, most probably triggered by his mother being diagnosed with cancer.

As Janey underwent a double mastectomy and then chemotherapy for a particularly aggressive form of breast cancer, Dom became a limpet, hanging onto his mother. But not to support her, or help her. Not to make her comfortable, or to try and get her to eat. Oh no, all he wanted was money to feed his habit. To start with she did help him. She gave him hundreds of pounds. But when she refused to give him anymore, telling him she didn't have it, he started to steal from her.

Her jewellery began to disappear. Money would be gone from her purse that she didn't remember spending. A particularly fine piece of china was suddenly not in the display cabinet. Those horrible acts weighed on Janey's mind and dragged her down. It took the energy she should have been using to fight the cancer and sapped her resolve.

The Whisperer had given up his job as a prison officer to look after her. It had taken six months for her to die. Six agonising months, during which time her son should have been there for her. Not in town buying drugs, or passed out in some decrepit flat with his junkie mates.

Once Janey had died and left him alone, the Whisperer felt as though his world had collapsed. He had no job, no wife and no money and if he wasn't able to get a job, he'd have no house. He couldn't get a permanent post back at the prison. Budget restrictions, cut backs, re-organisation, whatever they called it, it meant no job. But they did offer temporary work, to cover illness, holidays, that sort of thing. He applied to other prisons in the area, who also offered him temporary contracts. So he filled his days and mostly nights in several different prisons.

And as for Dom? The Whisperer had made sure Dom knew what he thought of him. He was a bloody good for nothing, waste of space, disgusting junkie, unloved, unwanted and better off dead. And that's exactly what happened. Dom died. They said it was a drug overdose, but the Whisperer knew better. Dom had committed suicide because he couldn't bear the truth. The truth that he'd caused his mother's death. The truth that the Whisperer had made sure he knew.

The passing of Dom gave the Whisperer a modicum of comfort. He had passed judgment on Dom and his suicide made the Whisperer feel that justice had been done. And after all, wasn't that what he was doing now? He made the prisoners face the consequences of their actions. And if they couldn't live with themselves after that, then that was just fine by him. After all they had the right to decide whether they lived or died. Didn't they?

Ten

The custody van arrived at Reading Young Offenders Institute, after picking up a prisoner from the local Magistrate's Court cells. It was just before 6pm. Sean, the sole occupant of the van, lurched in his seat as the vehicle came to a stop. As he waited, he could hear the large gates of the prison grating closed behind the van. A sound that terrified him, for it confirmed that he was really being incarcerated. It wasn't a bad dream. It was all too real. After being unlocked, Sean was led out of the plastic cubicle he'd been travelling in by a guard and guided into the prison.

He was led into a windowless room to wait. For what, he didn't know. He scratched at his unruly brown hair. It was normally teased into a fashionable sweep across his head and forehead, à la a member of a famous boy band. But since his arrest, appearance at the Magistrates Court and subsequent drive to Reading Young Officers Institute, it had turned into nothing more stylish than a bird's nest. He looked down at his hands. They weren't shaking, yet. But his foot tapped unchecked on the lino-covered floor.

A door opening made him jump and jerk around to

see who was there. An older lady, about his mum's age, walked in carrying a clipboard. She was dressed in what he supposed was a prison officer's uniform, white shirt with epaulets, dark trousers, large belt, chain, a bunch of keys and a name tag. He couldn't see what the tag said her name was and to be honest he didn't really care.

"Right," she said, sitting herself at the table with Sean. "What's your name and date of birth?"

Sean was sure she knew it already, but gave her the information she requested, struggling to get the words out through his frozen lips and clammy mouth. He sat quietly while she completed her paperwork. But he couldn't seem to stop his foot tapping. It appeared to have a life of its own. The officer was reading stuff clipped to her board. He guessed it was the reasons behind his arrival, but he didn't ask and she didn't volunteer any information.

Once she'd finished, she nodded at him and opened the reception room door. A burly man walked into the room and grabbed Sean's elbow. Sean looked from one to the other, not knowing what was going on, feeling as though his chest might burst with fright. He was led into another room and told to remove his white sweatshirt, as the officer needed to search him. Sean duly complied with hands that were now shaking. He had no idea what was going on or why they were making him strip.

"Now your trousers," the man said, without giving Sean his sweatshirt back.

Sean obeyed, taking off his trainers and pulling his jeans and socks off, hobbling on one foot as the other got stuck in the material. Dressed only in his boxers he was then led to a strange chair.

"Sit there, lad, while we scan you."

"Scan me," Sean managed to squeak, then flushing red, embarrassed by his fear and lack of control over his voice.

"Yes, just in case you've got anything concealed about your person."

Sean sat in the large grey plastic chair, wondering what on earth the officer was talking about. He had no clothes on, apart from his flimsy boxers, so he was thoroughly bemused by the procedure.

"Where?" he asked the officer.

"Where what?"

"Where would I hide something?"

"Ah, your first time inside is it?"

Sean nodded his reply.

"Just ask the lads on the wing, they'll tell you all about it. Highly resourceful some of them are, makes my eyes water to think about it. Right, up you get and put these on."

Sean took the white tee-shirt, grey sweatshirt and sweat pants from the officer.

"You can keep your trainers," he said as he packed Sean's old clothes away into a plastic storage box that had Sean's picture, name and prison number taped to the lid. With a jolt that felt like he'd been struck with lightening, Sean suddenly understood that everything that was happening to him was real. It wasn't a bad dream. He looked at the strange clothing, which felt dry and coarse against his skin and bit his lip in an effort to stop crying.

"Finished, Clive?" The female prison officer was back.

"Yep, all yours," the man replied. Then he said to Sean, "Off you go then."

"Where to?"

"The Remand wing. Here, take this with you."

Sean took a transparent plastic bag that had a towel in. He also caught sight of a couple of pairs of underwear. On unsteady legs he followed the woman through the prison, stopping at each gate for her to unlock and then relock it. Sean's first glimpse of the Remand wing was of a large number of prisoners milling around, all dressed in the same grey garb as he was, only differentiated by the trainers they wore. He shrunk away from them, trying to use the prison officer as a shield. Looking up, he saw the wing was on two levels, ground floor and first floor. There were large metal steps up to the higher level that they were now climbing. At the top, Sean looked down on the safety net slung under the rectangular void. A grim reminder of how some people were affected by being incarcerated.

"Come on," she called seemingly oblivious to his fear, "I'll show you your cell."

As they walked along the landing, Sean was pushed forward and made to walk in front of her.

"It's this one, come on," she said and unlocked a huge metal door with a key from her chain. Sean couldn't take his eyes of the door. He was drawn to it like a moth to a flame. How would he survive behind that? It was so large, so solid, so intimidating. His legs wobbled and the plastic bag he was carrying slipped from his grasp.

Once the door was opened he saw the inside of the cell. He looked at the bed, on which was a yellowing stained duvet and pillow; on top of the bedding had been placed a stash of sweets and chocolate bars and a carton of drink. The cell was narrow and confined and as well as the bed contained a toilet without a seat. Sean had never felt so depressed. Even the glimpse of an old fashioned television set on a desk didn't cheer him up. After picking his plastic bag up from the floor and placing it on the bed, he was told to once again follow the prison officer.

In yet another windowless room, Sean met yet another officer. He was very confused and frightened of them all. He had no idea who they all were or what they did. All he could see was the chain and bunch of keys that they all had attached to their belts.

"Hi, Sean, sit down, I'm Pat. I've just a few questions for you."

"Why?" he asked, sitting down as he was told.

"So we can get to know you and work out the best way to help you."

"Help me?"

"Yes and I'll explain some of the rules."

Ah, rules. There were always rules, he thought. Of course, he had no choice but to answer her questions. But the first one she asked gave him a shock.

"Have you had any feelings of self harm or suicide?"

"Eh?" Sean thought the question bizarre. "Um, no, why would I?"

But she didn't answer.

"Who do you live with?"

"My mum, why?"

The prison officer continued her irritating habit of answering his question with a question of her own.

"How are things with your mum? Does she know you're here?"

"Of course she does, why wouldn't she?" Sean was becoming ever more disturbed. He felt himself beginning to panic and his foot beat a rapid tattoo on the floor.

"Do you have any medical conditions we should be aware of?"

"No. Can I phone my girlfriend?"

Sean desperately wanted to chew at his finger, but he thought that might show the woman officer that he was intimidated by her questions, so he sat on his hands, forgetting that his foot was still tapping away and calling attention to his distress.

"How do you feel about being here at Reading?"

That question confirmed Sean's suspicion that the woman was mad.

"How do you think I'm feeling? What a bloody stupid question. What happens now? Am I going to be locked in? Can I watch TV? Can I keep the lights on?"

At last Pat put her pen down and looked up at Sean.

"I'm sorry, I should have answered your questions," she said. "You can make a phone call once we've organised a phone card for you, so that won't happen until tomorrow. You'll have to let us have a list of the phone numbers you want to ring, for approval. You can watch TV and yes, you are going to be locked in. But you can keep the light on. There's a switch in your cell for you to turn it off when you're ready to sleep. Compulsory lights out is at 2am when they go off automatically. Alright? I think that will do for now. There'll be various inductions over the coming week and the Chaplain has been booked to come and see you tomorrow. You can go to your cell now."

Sean wanted to scream at her that no, everything wasn't alright. He didn't think anything would ever be alright again. He wanted to go home. He sat there hoping he would soon wake up from this terrible nightmare and find himself back in his bedroom.

Eleven

Karen Smith looked around the visitor's room that was already crowded. It was pouring down with rain outside, which had turned the atmosphere in the room into the inside of a tropical greenhouse. It was like walking through the Eden Project, but without the high glass ceiling. The combination of the heating and around 30 people in the room all sat in damp clothing had produced a hot house effect, with people quietly steaming as they sat and chatted.

Scanning the tables, she saw girlfriends grasping the hand of boyfriends, mothers proudly showing off their children and mothers and fathers, just like herself, with concern and worry etched in their faces. She was sure she looked just the same as them, so she re-arranged her face when she saw her son and plastered on what she hoped was a happy smile.

"How are you, Sean?" she asked, quickly taking a seat. She went to dump her handbag on the floor, an automatic gesture and then realised she didn't have one with her. It had been taken from her, as had her phone and anything else she'd stuffed in her pockets. They weren't meeting in a cafe, but in the Visitor Centre at

HMYOI Reading.

"I'm great, mum," he replied.

"Honestly?" Karen looked closely at his face for signs of lying, but his eyes were clear, his face fresh and his hair newly washed. Maybe he was telling the truth.

"Is there any news?" she asked, brushing her damp locks off her face.

"Yeah, my solicitor reckons it's a slam dunk." At her frown, he explained, "I've got a good case, he's confident I'll be out in a few weeks. Acquitted, no less. So no worries."

"Are you keeping busy?"

"So, so, there's not much to do really as I'm on remand, but we get more privileges because of it, so I've a television and I've bought some stuff from the canteen. Did you bring those books for me?"

"Yes, I've left them with the officer. You should get them later today."

"Thanks, mum, there's not much science fiction in the library here. And the money?"

"Don't worry, I've paid that in to your canteen account."

"Thanks, mum, having money for basics and tobacco really makes a difference."

"You could have given up smoking instead," Karen tried a joke and hoped he didn't take it the wrong way.

"Yeah, right, easier said than done. Maybe when I get out, eh?"

"Yes, maybe," she agreed. "So you seemed to have settled in alright?"

"Guess so. Luckily I was put in with a great bloke who showed me round, told me the routine. You know, what to do and not to do. I was scared bloody stiff at the start. The first night... well, let's just say being here is not as bad as my imagination made it out to be. And my solicitor being hopeful of getting me out, has helped. Anyway," Sean moved around on his seat as though trying to get comfortable, "tell me your news. What's going on at home?"

They spent the next half an hour chatting amicably, whilst having a drink and eating a chocolate bar from the vending machines. She wasn't sure if Sean would want to talk about Candice, so she deliberately didn't mention her. Candice was his girlfriend who he'd had underage sex with. She was 15 years old when they met and Sean was 17. Neither had thought anything about their ages, until her father found out about their relationship. Karen hadn't known the girl's age and never asked. To her modern girls all looked older than they probably were. It seemed tight fitting sexy clothes, make up and high heels were the norm these days.

The time with her son was over all too soon and the call that visiting time was over, brought unbidden tears to her eyes.

"Hey, mum, don't do that," pleaded Sean.

"Sorry, love," and Karen did her best to brighten up. She didn't want Sean worrying over her tears. She had to show him she could be strong too. "Don't worry, I'm fine," she reassured him and made a point of smiling and waving to him from the doorway. But inside her heart was breaking.

Twelve

"Are you sure you should go in today?" Billy's concern was evident in his open, handsome, fresh face as he looked at Emma.

She was putting on her black trouser suit, teamed with a black and white blouse. The blouse had buttons down the back, rather than the front, so no one would get an unintentional glimpse of her cleavage, or worse still, her breasts. She glanced in the mirror at the very unattractive red skin around her nose and chapped lips and promptly sneezed.

Through a tissue held against her face, she said, "Billy, I've got to. We're so understaffed with this cold that's going round. As it is I'm going to have to help with supervision at lunch time. The lads are to be banged up all afternoon because we won't have enough officers for recreation. At the very least they should have a break at lunch."

Billy put his hands on her shoulders and pulled her towards him. "Don't do too much or you'll find yourself in bed with flu, or worse, if you're not careful."

Emma nodded her agreement. "Promise," she whispered and went to kiss him.

He moved backwards rapidly. "On the cheek, please, I don't want your germs!"

Emma laughed and kissed his cheek as requested and reached up to tousle his blond hair, before leaving their house in Wokingham to drive to work.

As she passed the front of their rented house in her Mini Cooper, Emma remembered her bedsit, where she had lived before, with a small smile. She'd loved that little flat in the basement of a large Victorian house, but since she and Billy had become a couple, both felt that because of their hectic work schedules, it was best to live together, reasoning that if they didn't and kept separate homes in Wokingham and Aldershot, they'd hardly ever see one another. Billy was Sgt Billy Williams, of the Royal Military Police, Special Investigations Branch, based at Provost Barracks on Aldershot Garrison.

A sneezing fit brought her back to the present, her illness reminding her that she also wanted to see the Medical Officer. Not because of her cold, but because of the state of some of the lads. Too many of them seemed to be self-harming and she wanted to know what he was doing to find out the reasons behind their outward display of despair.

Emma thought back to her original goal when joining the staff at Reading HMYOI, to get as many lads in her care as possible interested in education. That was a bit of a pipedream at the moment. It seemed that all she was doing these days was talking to very unhappy, depressed inmates about how best to get them through the days without doing anything stupid to themselves. She spent more time filling out forms and requisitions that no one seemed to read or take any notice of, than she did talking to the boys and trying to work out what was best for them going forward.

An hour or so later, at the Governor's morning briefing, the overriding topic was concern over the prison officer ratio to prisoners, due to the unforeseen medical emergency.

The Governor wanted an update as to staff numbers. "What say you, Chief?" he asked Chief Robinson. The Governor smoothed down his tie with one hand and picked up a pen with the other. Emma was sure she hadn't seen that tie before, so it must be yet another new one. It seemed the Governor was living up to his reputation as a sharp dresser.

"Well, Governor, whilst I have to admit we are 25% down on officers on the wings, I've moved them around so we have equal coverage on all four wings. Even if the officer numbers are lower than usual," he began.

Chief Robinson always sat to attention and today was no different. His back was rigid and his arms placed on the table, a file in between them. He hadn't needed to refer to his file. As usual he was word perfect in his report. Emma wondered how many times he practiced his little speeches before the meeting.

"Is anyone else able to come in?" the Governor asked, breaking into Emma's thoughts about Chief Robinson.

"Well, sir, I'm shying away of allowing officers to pull double shifts. A tired officer can be as bad as no officer."

"I don't think that's quite what the Governor wanted to know," Emma put her oar in.

Chief Robinson bristled and said, "I can assure everyone," and he looked pointedly at Emma, "that there is no possible danger of an incident as I've managed to locate some men who have previously worked here, to fill in on a temporary supply basis."

"Excellent, Chief," said the Governor.

"Who are these men, Chief?" Emma wanted to know.

But was she shot down with a curt, "That's an operational matter," by Chief Robinson, who was backed up by Chad Albright, nodding his head vigorously in response to Robinson's glare.

"Surely the safety of everyone in the prison is the responsibility of all staff, not just the remit of the Chief and Head of Operations," she said.

"Oh, in that case are you going to put a uniform back on then and come and work on the wings?" the Chief sneered at her.

"I think that's enough, Chief," the Governor intervened. "All staff are providing as much cover as they can, particularly at lunch-time and tea-time. I don't think attacking each other is the best way forward. Do you?"

Everyone mumbled, "No Governor," in suitably chastised tones.

"I rather think things are getting a bit heated," he said. "But I am sure it's because everyone has the safety of all the prisoners at heart. Don't you?" he glared at everyone around the table, as if daring anyone to refute the statement.

Chief Robinson glowered at Emma. Emma stared at the Chief and Chad Albright. The Medical Officer looked down at his notes and Father Batty sat there with steepled fingers and a bemused look on his face.

After the meeting broke up, Emma walked down the corridor with the Medical Officer. Geoff Fox looked as if he was under more pressure than the others who were at the meeting. Emma supposed that was because not only had he the prisoners who were coming down with the cold to deal with, but the lock-down was affecting the more vulnerable prisoners. His face was pinched and wan and his eyes red and watering.

"Are you alright, Geoff," Emma asked as they walked through the corridors of power.

"I'll be fine," he said, sniffing.

"Looks like you're succumbing to this cold as well," she said, then scrabbling in her pocket, promptly sneezed into a tissue.

"You and me both," he smiled weakly.

"How are the lads holding up?" Emma stopped walking, to signal this was not a light hearted chit chat.

Geoff Fox stopped and stood beside her. "Honestly?"

"Yes, Geoff, honestly."

"I've no bloody idea. At the moment I'm running to simply stand still. In other words, I'm getting nowhere fast."

"It's the most vulnerable that bother me," said Emma.

"I agree, but what can I do? The hospital wing is full, I've a long line of lads to see every morning and evening. If there are those suffering mentally from being locked up for so many hours a day, I've no idea. And I won't have, unless the wing officers notify me."

"And the wings don't have enough officers on duty to worry about that sort of problem," Emma said.

"Exactly," Geoff agreed. "If you get any bright ideas that would solve the conundrum, do let me know, won't you," and he walked off, blowing his nose loudly into his handkerchief.

Thirteen

Connor picked up his book, glanced at it, then put it down again. Walked over and turned his TV on. Flicked through the channels, then turned it off again. Lying down on his bunk, he put his hands underneath his head, then after a moment got up again, savagely blinking away tears of self-pity. He walked over to his desk, sat in his chair and looked at the two empty bunks. One of them belonged to Chris, his mate. But Chris wasn't here. He'd succumbed to the flu bug and was in the hospital wing. His cough had turned into bronchitis and there was concern about the possibility of pneumonia. The screws thought it best to keep those suffering from such infections segregated. He could understand it, really, them trying to keep a lid on the germs in an attempt to stop them spreading. But it wasn't working. It was difficult to say if there were more screws ill than inmates. All you could hear up and down the landing were sneezes, blowing of noses, hawking of phlegm and coughing. Underneath all that were the usual sounds of a prison: gates slamming; locks turning; keys jingling; people shouting. It was doing his head in.

So was being locked in his cell on his own, because that's when the voices came. They spoke to him making his head pound and his skull feel like it was splitting.

His mum: 'Don't you know you've broken my heart?'

His dad: 'You lazy good for nothing.'

His employer: 'I trusted you and all you did in return was steal from me!'

His girlfriend: 'What am I supposed to do now? How am I supposed to cope with no money and a kid to look after?'

His son: 'Daddy don't leave me!'

His dad: 'Don't think you'll be able to get a job when you come out. Not after what you've done. Drinking like that. Getting in a fight. Hurting someone. Not to mention stealing the money to pay for your drunken binge in the first place.'

His aunt: 'Broken your mum's heart you have.'

His girlfriend: 'Don't think I'll wait for you. I'm a woman. I've got needs.'

What sort of needs she meant didn't bear thinking about.

His employer: 'You'll never get a reference out of me for another job. I wouldn't wish you on my worst enemy!'

Connor wouldn't wish himself on his worst enemy either. He dashed away more tears. He was so fed up of crying all the time. Being so depressed. But what was there to be happy about? He was stuck in here for five years. Five bloody years for grievous bodily harm! Five years for a moment of madness. He'd never make it. He knew that. He wasn't strong enough.

"Alright in there, Connor, are you?" a soft voice came whispering through the door. "Thought I heard you crying. Crying like a baby. Like the baby you are. Crying for your family are you? Well, you've lost them now, haven't you?"

"Who are you? What do you want?" Connor screamed then pressed his hands over his ears, so he couldn't hear the taunts of the Whisperer from the other side of the door.

But the whispering continued and Connor was no longer sure if the voice was real or a figment of his imagination.

"No one wants you now, do you they? No one wants a thief or a bully for a son, for a boyfriend, for a father. They'd all be better off without you. You know that, don't you? Why don't you do them a favour and top yourself. Get one thing right in your life for once."

Connor screamed, "Go away, go away!" and threw himself on his bunk, scrabbling into the far corner and covering his head with his blanket. "Leave me alone," he sobbed, but the words that had been whispered at the door, were now echoing inside his head.

The only thing that kept the voices away was his home-made knife. He'd fashioned it out of a razor blade and hidden it in his mattress. Pulling it along his arm, or along his thigh helped. If he concentrated hard on the pain, on the blood that oozed from the cut, then he found he could keep a clear head. He held the blade in his hand, as a believer would hold a cross. It was the only thing left to him now, the only thing that made a difference.

He stayed huddled under his blanket, his shiv close to him, while he decided what to do for the best.

Fourteen

The shrill bell echoed along the wing. It was lunch-time. Emma walked along the upper tier, cajoling the lads along with a quiet word here and a shout there. A joke shared or an abusive term batted away. Some of the lads were slow to emerge from the cell where they had been banged up all morning. They shuffled out of the door, still in a half trance, rubbing sleep out of their eyes.

"Come on you lot, look lively," Emma shouted. "Anyone would think it was breakfast, not the middle of the day."

"To what do we owe this honour, miss?" someone shouted. "Not seen you down on the wing for a while."

"Blame it on this bug, Jason," Emma called. "Enjoy my company while you can, I'll be gone again before you know it."

"Like a fucking genie, you are, miss," someone called.

"Oh, you mean I'm not princess material?" asked Emma.

"You can be my princess any day!"

"Sorry, Sean, I've already got a handsome prince,"

Emma laughed. "Now go on with you, I hear there's something special on the menu today."

"Yeah, salmonella to go with the E.Coli!" and the lads laughed as they made their way downstairs, clanging down the mental rungs.

Emma paused outside a partly opened door. "Come on," she called walking into the cell. "Lunch will be cold unless you get a move on."

In the far corner of a bunk, she could just make out something huddled under a blanket. Was it a person? Or someone who'd made a mess of their bed and not tidied it up. She strode over to the bunk and pulled at the blanket.

"Come, on, up you get," she said, hoping she wasn't about to make a fool of herself by talking to a load of bedding and pillows.

She opened her mouth to speak again, but instead of words, a scream came out, filling the small space. Clamping her hand over her mouth to stop both the scream and the last coffee she'd drunk spewing out, she ran for the door and pressed the emergency button on the outside of the cell, making a note of the cell number as she did so. Going back inside she screamed into her radio, "Get the doctor to cell 21 now! One of the lads has slit his wrists, there's blood everywhere!"

Actually that was an understatement to say he'd slit his wrists. It looked like he had stuck a knife into every place on his body where he could get to an artery. The stab wounds were still oozing blood making her wonder if he was still alive, if there was any chance of saving him. He was on the bottom bunk, so she stooped down and pulled at his legs, his body now lying down flat on the mattress. She wanted to check if he was alive, but he'd stabbed his neck and wrists at the pulse points. She put her head on his chest to see if she could hear his heartbeat, but the cacophony of noise from the alarm, officers shouting, lads shouting and pounding feet made the task impossible. She tried to feel for any imperceptible rise and fall of his chest, but it was impossible to tell if he was breathing or not.

A clatter of feet arrived at the door and Emma turned and shouted, "Help me get him off this bunk."

Emma grabbed the lad's feet while an officer grabbed the boy under the arms. Together they placed him on the floor, where Emma immediately began administering CPR, pushing against the boy's breastbone with her clasped hands. She must have subliminally remembered the latest adverts on television showing people how to administer CPR. Clasped hands on the chest and pump to the rhythm of The Bee Gee's record, 'Staying Alive'.

"Where's the fucking doctor?" she shouted, all the while maintaining her rhythm.

"Here," said a voice by her ear. "You can stop that now, Emma."

"No I can't."

"Emma, you have to, I need to examine him," said Geoff Fox.

But Emma couldn't seem to stop her hands pumping the boy's chest and someone had to grab her shoulders and prise her off him.

She struggled against the strong arms, but she wasn't powerful enough to wrench out of the man's grip and she was lifted up onto her feet and swung out of the way. She looked down at the boy and then at the doctor. Maybe the boy was still alive? Could they save him? But Geoff shook his head and closed the boy's eyes.

"I don't even know his name," said Emma. "What's his name? Come on, what's his name?" she looked around at the officers crowded into the cell. "Someone must know his bloody name!"

Fifteen

The Governor's daily briefing the next morning was a very sombre affair. After the usual operational matters he requested background information on the boy who had died. Emma had found out his name. He was called Connor Reece and had been just 19 years of age. He was in prison for grievous bodily harm. He had caused a fight with someone for no apparent reason, whilst drinking in public. The poor innocent victim he'd beaten up had been left with broken bones, severe bruising and lost his spleen. Apparently it was a wonder he hadn't died.

Geoff Fox continued his background report on Connor and said, "It appears he had a history of solvent and alcohol abuse, stretching back to when he was 10 years old."

"Was he put into care?" Emma asked, flicking through the paperwork she had to try and find the answer to her own question.

"No, his mother and father are both alive, so he lived with them until he was 18."

"And how did that work out?" Emma stopped looking through her papers and looked up at Geoff Fox.

"Not very well, I'm afraid. They couldn't cope with him and he basically took no notice of them. He was allocated a Social Worker, but he was only seen sporadically. Connor regularly missed appointments or wasn't in when she called round to the house to try and find him."

"What else does the social worker's report on him say?" asked the Governor. Emma felt he spoke just a little too eagerly, wanting to blame Connor's background for the suicide and not the establishment.

"As well as substance abuse, he regularly self-harmed."

"Jesus," whispered Emma. What a mess the boy's life had been, she realised. If only they'd had that information when he arrived at Reading, maybe things would have turned out differently.

"But that's not all," said Geoff and Emma wondered what could be worse than a teenager who had a history of substance abuse and self harm.

"According to her report, he left his parent's house and moved in with his girlfriend who'd had his son. He found the responsibility too much to cope with and couldn't keep down a job. But he also had a fear of being left alone and had warned that he would kill himself if he was ever returned to prison."

"Returned to prison?"

"Yes, he was given six days just a few weeks ago."

"What had he done to get six days?" Emma couldn't imagine such a short sentence would have been worth handing down.

"He didn't have a television licence for the telly in the flat," Geoff finished and started to play with the pens in the top pocket of his white coat.

Emma was speechless. She had to brush away a tear that had squeezed out of her eye and was threatening to roll down her cheek.

"Emma," the Governor called her back from her emotional black hole.

"Yes, Governor?"

"Had Connor been referred to you?"

"No, Governor."

Sharp closed his eyes briefly in response to her answer. Then collecting himself said, "Geoff? What about you? Did you know all this? Had he been referred to you?"

"No, Governor. I only got all this information from contacting his Social Worker directly yesterday, after Connor had died."

"Chief Robinson, did the wing have any information on him?"

"No, Governor. We had no idea he was a high risk inmate."

"Christ," said the Governor, running his fingers through his normally immaculate hair that once again was falling over his forehead. "Connor didn't just fall through the cracks he fell down a bloody sink hole. I want a full investigation into this case. The Coroner will want it anyway, so we may as well be prepared. We failed him in life so let's make sure we don't fail him in death."

"Yes, Governor," they all responded.

After the meeting broke up, Emma wandered back to her office, her mind on the Governor's words. She wasn't sure how sincere they were which she knew was an awful thing to think. But with Governor Sharp she always got the impression that any investigation was all about covering his own back, whilst outwardly spouting empty platitudes. It seemed every outside agency he could think of would be accused of failing Connor, but definitely not Reading HMYOI. For how could they have failed Connor when they'd known nothing about him?

Sixteen

When she got home that night, Emma was grateful that Billy had made it back from Aldershot Garrison, even though he was in the middle of a big investigation. Luckily she'd thrown the ingredients for a casserole into the slow cooker that morning, so she didn't have to prepare a meal. It was already made. She poured herself a glass of wine and Billy a beer and they sat down in the comfortable lounge and chatted before eating, while they waited for a garlic baguette to heat up. They had Channel Four news on the television with the volume turned down low, neither of them taking much notice of it.

"Well, how did it go today?" Billy asked, as they sat on the large squashy sofa that Emma had insisted on buying when they'd set up house together, even though they couldn't really afford it at the time. Sighing and settling back amongst the cushions, she told him about the Governor's meeting that morning.

"I'm really beginning to wonder if I can do this job," she concluded.

"Hey," Billy said, putting his arm around her. "That's not the attitude I expected from you."

"But I don't think I can cope with losing two boys in as many months," Emma shook her head. "What if there's more?"

Billy sat up straight and turned to face her. "Look, even though there have been two suicides, you aren't personally responsible for either of them. You know that."

"Well, I feel as if I am. My remit is inmate welfare."

"I know, but let's take Connor. Firstly, he has to take some responsibility for his actions. Secondly, who was involved in his life? His parents have to take some responsibility for the way they brought him up. Okay so the system failed this lad. But how many does it save? Surely the ones you all save are enough to outweigh the ones you don't."

"I don't know about that."

But it seemed Billy wasn't to be deflected and he pressed on. "Look at all the good you do. Think about it. If you walk away now, boys will still die, maybe more than if you stay. I know it's a dreadful thing when someone is so upset that they take their own life. You can't get away from that. But you need to look for the small things you do that make the difference."

"Is that how you deal with being a military policeman?"

"That's a bit different," said Billy after taking a gulp of his beer. "Being in the SIB I take the worst offenders and clean them out of the army. The uniformed military police are the ones that do the little things that make a difference."

"Okay, come on then, what are those little things?"

"Having a quiet word, instead of nicking someone. Or nicking someone for a minor offence, to stop them from doing something far worse. Look, if you think about it, you are all working towards keeping Reading HMYOI a safer place for those who are there for whatever reason. You can't undo what the individuals have done that got them incarcerated in the first place, but you can all try and make a difference to them while they are there. And give them a better chance of making a go of it on the outside, when they're released."

"Are we all working towards that though, Billy?" Emma asked as she picked up her glass and gazed thoughtfully into the contents. "The Governor seems more interested in the bigger picture. The administration side of the job. The management of the establishment. I can't remember the last time he actually met a prisoner, let alone had a conversation with one. The Medical Officer, Geoff, is so overworked it's unreal. He's been pleading for more nurses, but none have ever materialised. Father Batty does what he can, but all he can offer is spiritual comfort and organise the Prison Visitors. Chief Robinson is so old school, it's ridiculous. He's ex-army and acts like he's still in uniform."

"Was he a Regimental Sgt Major?"

"How did you know that?" said Emma.

"Because that's what a lot of the Sergeants and Sgt Majors from training facilities go on to do. When they retire from the army, they join the Prison Service."

"Well, sometimes he forgets where he is and shouts at the boys like they're on a parade ground or undergoing physical training."

Billy grinned. "I'm sure he means well."

"He might do, but I'm not sure all of his officers do."

"Eh?"

Emma put down her glass before speaking. "It's just

something some of the lads have been saying, at least the more vulnerable ones have. Apparently someone talks to them through the cell doors, at night usually."

"Really?"

"Yes. He says vile, horrible things apparently. He taunts them and goads them so they feel so bad that they are self harming, or worse. They call him the Whisperer."

"My God, have you told anyone?" Billy seemed as dismayed by this piece of information as Emma was and he ran his hand through his blond hair, scratching at his scalp.

"No, because the first time I heard about it, I thought this Whisperer was a figment of the boy's imagination. Some of these lads are seriously mentally ill, Billy. You can't always take what they say as gospel. But since then, a couple of other lads have mentioned it to me, including the boy in the cell next to Connor."

"Well you're going to have to report it to the Governor, aren't you?"

"I was hoping to get something concrete, something more than rumours and Chinese whispers, before I went to him. It might not be an officer."

"Then that's something you're going to have to find out, isn't it. You can't walk away now and let Jimmy and Connor down. Find out what's going on. You're ballsy enough. If you really feel there's a problem officer, get to the bottom of it. You owe it to them."

Billy poured her more wine and handed her the glass.

"To Jimmy and Connor," he said raising his beer to her wine and they both took a large gulp of their drinks.

Seventeen

The Whisperer turned off the local television news, a gloating smile lighting up his frog-like features. His eyes bulged more than normal and he flicked his tongue across his lips. There had been another suicide. My God he was getting good at this. He walked out of the living room and up the steep stairs, trailing his hand along the bumpy raised pattern of the wall paper as he went. He headed along the landing to the loft hatch. Grabbing the pole hanging on the wall, he hooked it into the ring on the trap door and pulled. A metal ladder dropped down and unfolded and once he had locked it into place he climbed up it. Poking his head through the hole, he felt around with his hand on the loft floor. At last it brushed over a large diary. Pulling it through the hole, he climbed down again, the book clasped to his chest with one arm.

When he reached the bottom of the ladder, he looked at his book, then at the open hatch, trying to make his mind up. Should he should leave the hatch open, or close it? Deciding that he would spend some time looking over his past successes as well as writing up this new one, The Whisperer pushed the ladder back into the hatch and hung the pole back on the wall.

Once downstairs, he poured himself a beer and went into the sitting room. Placing the book and the beer on the coffee table in front of the settee, he sat down and then passed his hands reverently over his diary, as though it were a bible, which, of course, it was to him in a way. It was a detailed history of his whisperings and how they had affected his subjects. Prisons were proving to be a fertile hunting ground. After all, the men and women he came across in the establishments he worked in were sitting targets. They couldn't get away from him. They were forced to listen. There was nowhere to hide from him in a cell. There were a few young men in Reading Young Offenders Institute who were particularly vulnerable, making them, on the whole, open to his suggestions. He was still working on them. It would be a little while yet before they found their way into the annals of his ledger.

He looked over his entries on Jimmy Hill. He'd made detailed notes on the boy's history, snatches of which he'd picked up from staff on the wing, or from gossip overheard during recreation, as well as from briefings. He'd detailed the days, times and content of his whisperings, then recorded the inevitable conclusion - the time and manner of Jimmy's death.

The Whisperer picked up his fountain pen, found the correct page and began to write Connor's entry.

Eighteen

Emma knocked on Chief Robinson's door. "Have you a minute, Chief?"

"Is it urgent, Miss Harrison? I'm trying to arrange supply cover. I've still got a few officers off with this cold." Chief Robinson continued to look down at the papers strewn across his desk.

"I just wondered what your thoughts were on the increase in suicides in the establishment?"

Her words made him look up at her. "I wouldn't imagine that is a topic for a quick conversation," he said.

Emma moved into the Chief's office and leaned on the wall next to the open door, rather than sitting down. She was hoping her casual pose would entice him to talk to her.

"Seriously, Chief, what do you make of it? I'd value your opinion."

"There's nothing to make of anything," the Chief sighed, putting down his pen. "It happens. It's a fact of life in the Prison Service. Some of the kids just can't hack it. That may sound harsh, but there it is. There's no point in being sentimental about it. Statistically speaking, there will be suicides in prisons."

"You don't think there's more to it than that? More behind the suicides than just statistics?"

"What on earth would give you that idea?"

Emma paused for a moment, chewing the inside of her cheek, summoning up her courage. "Let's, say you're right. But have you thought about the procedures we have in place?"

"What are you talking about now, Miss Harrison? I really do have to get on."

The Chief's failure to use her name, still grated on Emma and she had to push away the anger that was building inside, constricting her chest, making it hard to breathe.

"The procedures we have in place for those who self-harm. Are they robust enough? Are protocols being adhered to by all staff?" She realised she was beginning to sound as pompous as Robinson himself.

"Look, Miss Harrison. You should know better, after all you have been in the Service nearly three years. Haven't you realised by now that most of the lads who self-harm are just vying for attention? When the wings are over-crowded and we are under-staffed, most of them are ignored. They don't get the attention they think they warrant. So they self-harm. That way we have to take some notice of them. Most of the time they just want to be moved away from a hated cell mate, or want to work in a different place, or even attend one of your precious education courses. They've put their forms in but nothing has happened. So they get frustrated with the system and do something to bring themselves to our attention."

"Are you sure of that?"

"Yes." His tone was emphatic, as if daring her to

challenge him. So she did.

"Well, I'm not," said Emma pushing herself off the wall. "We need to learn from each suicide. Make sure the lads who are mentally ill get the treatment they deserve."

"And you think the lads who self harm are mentally ill?"

"Yes. I agree it's a cry for help. But they do it because they are ill, not just because they want another bloody blanket."

Constantly banging her head against the immovable object that was Chief Robinson meant that Emma was in danger of saying something she shouldn't, like calling him a dinosaur, or shouting that this wasn't the bloody army. But she swallowed, unclenched her fists and said in as normal a voice as she could manage, "I just think there's more behind these suicides than meets the eye. There have been rumours, Chief."

"Rumours?" At that, Robinson looked interested, or was it dismissive? She wasn't sure. She never was with him.

"Yes. Some of the lads are talking about someone whispering disparaging comments through the cell door at night."

"Disparaging comments? What are you talking about?"

"The voice ridicules them and is abusive."

"Miss Harrison, I really think you should go and do something constructive, rather than talking to me about rumours and such nonsense. I've got a mountain of paperwork to get through, never mind arranging cover for absent officers. Now if you'll excuse me..." and the Chief bent his head once more to the files on his desk.

Emma took the hint and left his office. But she

wasn't about to leave the subject. She'd just have to get some evidence. And the first place to start would be with those boys she was responsible for in her position as Assistant Governor for Inmate Welfare. The welfare of the boys was her concern and she wasn't about to let them down. No matter what Chief Robinson said or did.

Nineteen

Sean was late for the showers. He'd been reading one of the books his mum had brought in and become lost in the pages. When he realised what the time was, he grabbed his towel and shower gel and ran. He'd decided when he'd first been brought to Reading that the best way of keeping his spirits up was to look after himself. Keep clean, keep occupied and eat. Even if the food was disgusting, it was better than nothing. He also tried to keep as fit as possible by walking as much as he could during exercise and doing the odd push-up and stuff in his cell. His solicitor had been upbeat about an early release, as had his girlfriend, so he had to be as well.

He dodged around other prisoners as he walked as quickly as he could without drawing attention to himself. If he started running, he'd be in trouble, so he played by the rules and hurried. He clattered down the wing steps and heard the last call for the showers over the tannoy. Skidding on the wet tiles, he made it to the shower block just in time.

Quickly stripping off, he stood under the lukewarm water, nodding at a couple of lads who were just leaving. He was on his own and a small spike of fear pricked in his mind. But he told himself not to be so stupid and proceeded to wash his hair and then himself with the shower gel. He was just about to wash off the suds when a voice shouted, "Oy nonce, who said you could use the shower?"

Sean raised his head from the cascading water and looked at the boy in front of him. He was glaring at Sean and swinging around a sock. There was something in the toe of it which seemed hard and heavy, elongating the sock to at least twice its normal length.

"Don't know why you bother washing," another boy joined the first. "You'll never be able to wash the stink of nonce off. Can you still smell it, Col?"

"Reckon I can," the first boy said.

Sean was aware that both boys were playing with weighted socks, the material stretched from the weight in the toe. The one called Col, started swinging his sock around and took a step towards Sean, who shrank backwards to the tiled wall of the showers. But then he realised he had nowhere to go, as a third boy joined them. There was now one on either side of him and one in front. As they walked towards him, Sean tried to make a break for it, but slipped on the wet tiles and went down with a thump. He hit his elbow on the way down, but soon realised that injury was the least of his worries as socks filled with pool balls rained down on his unprotected body.

When it was over, Sean lay on the floor of the showers. The water sluicing away down the plug hole was now red, where there were once white suds. He sobbed quietly. He'd tried to tell them he wasn't a nonce. He hadn't gone with children. He didn't want anything to do with children. It's just that his girlfriend was only 15 when they'd met. But the more he'd protested, the more they'd hit him, so he'd stopped trying to make them see reason.

As he wept, he repeated her name to himself. She was 16 last month, his girlfriend, Candice. But her Dad had found out about them and reported Sean to the police. He didn't want to think his little girl was growing up. He didn't want her wasting her time on boys when she should be studying at school, especially with a boy who was older than her. So he'd taken his revenge by going to the police. Candice was livid and threatening to leave home. She was hoping to persuade her Dad to drop the charges, saying that otherwise he'd never see her again. She was confident she was going to make him change his mind. But it hadn't happened yet.

It seemed that telling his cell mate and another couple of lads that he'd been arrested for Unlawful Carnal Knowledge with an underage girl, had been the wrong thing to do. Someone must have said something to someone else and so it went on. That's how vicious rumours thrived in prison. The truth would have been distorted and now those three lads obviously viewed him as some sort of paedophile.

Sean tried to get up, but couldn't push himself off the floor. His arm didn't seem to work anymore and he slipped back down onto the cold, wet tiles, hoping someone would find him sooner rather than later.

Twenty

Emma hadn't forgotten about her intention to pursue the shadowy figure of the Whisperer. Needing to get concrete evidence of his existence, she had managed to get her hands on the staff rotas for the last three months from Joan. She had mumbled something about doing a project for the Governor and grabbed them and left the office, before Joan could question her.

Grasping the folder tightly to her, she made it to her office without being seen and closed the door behind her. Once inside, she relaxed a little and managed to smile at her own stupidity. She wasn't nearly important enough for anyone to think twice about what she might be doing. But on the other hand, she didn't want to be confronted either. A giggle escaped her lips. She felt like a spy.

Pulling herself together, she moved to sit at her desk and pulled towards her a notepad and pencil and opened the file containing the rotas. They were available on the establishment's intranet, but Emma didn't have security approval to look at them. Asking for that would have raised eyebrows. So she was stuck with the paper copies Joan printed off each week and kept in her office.

The problem was that the two recent suicides had been on different wings, so if there was a 'Whisperer', as the lads dubbed him, then surely it couldn't be anyone who was permanently on one wing. Also, she had to look at the days or even weeks leading up to the suicides. Plus the fact that there had been suicides earlier in the year, before she'd taken up her post and Emma had no idea if they were linked to the latest two or not. She wished she had more time to go over the paperwork, even take it home to look at it overnight, but she knew that to try and take unauthorised paperwork out of the establishment, would be foolish. So she bent her head to her task, needing to get the file back to Joan before anyone realised it was missing - particularly Chief Robinson or Chad Albright.

After a while, she sat back in her chair, pushed her glasses up her nose and went over her notes. There didn't seem to be any correlation between any officers and the suicides. Most of the officers were permanently on one particular wing, as it was felt that fostered good relations with the prisoners and instilled a sense of trust, by seeing the same faces every day. On the other hand, officers were also regularly swopped out to give them experience of other wings such as segregation or the hospital wing. Try as she might, she couldn't seem to find a pattern within the permanent staff. The only slight clue worth checking out, were the supply officers. Emma knew they were used during times of staffing problems due to holidays, sickness or injury and it seemed to her that leading up to the last four suicides there had been supply officers in the prison. However, the rotas didn't give names or details. She had no way of knowing if there were several officers or just one.

She made a note of the dates she was interested in and slipped the notepad into one of her desk drawers and locked it. Grabbing the file, she returned it to Joan with a breezy, "Thanks a lot," and made a quick exit.

Towards the end of the day, when Emma had finished her inmate interviews and after a meeting with the medical officer, she decided to take a walk on one of the wings and have a chat to some of the officers there about supply cover. She took with her a book she had promised Sean Smith, as an excuse.

Walking onto the wing, she headed over to the officer's station and was glad to see Tom Collins there, an officer she had worked with at a different establishment, when she was in uniform. He'd recently transferred to Reading, wanting a posting closer to his elderly parents. More importantly, Tom was an officer that had never seemed to resent her being on the graduate programme, at least not when she'd worked with him previously. He'd always said that being a Governor just wasn't for him and that he was much happier on the wings. He was a 'hands on' man and proud of it.

"Hey, Tom, how's things?"

"Oh, hi, Emma, not bad, you know."

"How are you all coping? Is everyone back from sick leave now?"

"Yes, thank God," said Tom. "Luckily a lot of the lads were ill at the same time, so things were quite quiet."

"Did you have any supply staff providing cover? Chief Robinson said he was drafted some in."

"Yeah, but that can be just as much of a pain as not having enough officers."

"Oh, really?" Emma said hoping to encourage him

to keep talking.

"Yes, they don't know the lads, the routines, that sort of stuff."

"But surely you must have regulars that cover?"

"Yeah, if we are lucky enough to get them, good supply officers are hard to find."

"So how many regularly work here?"

Emma saw Tom was looking at her suspiciously. It seemed she may have gone too far and had pushed too hard in her quest for information.

"Why would you want to know that?"

"Oh, no reason, just making conversation," she said.

"Why are you here, anyway?"

"Oh, right, I've come to see Sean Smith, I've a book I promised him," and Emma held it up against her chest like a shield. "So I guess I'll be off to see him now," she said and turned to leave.

"You could if he was here," said Tom.

She whirled around, "Why? Where's he gone?"

"I would have thought you'd have known, being in charge of inmate welfare." Tom paused and Emma got the distinct feeling that maybe Tom had changed his attitude towards her. "He's in the hospital wing," he said begrudgingly, "seems someone got to him in the showers."

Twenty One

Emma hurried to the hospital wing to see Sean. As she arrived, Geoff Fox was just leaving.

"Geoff, can I have a quick word?"

"Of course, but it will have to be here, I've got a meeting with the Governor and you know he doesn't like to be kept waiting."

"It's about Sean Smith. What happened?"

"He was found in the showers. It looks like he was set upon by a couple of guys, if not more. He hasn't any broken bones, but we're concerned about concussion, so we're keeping him overnight for observation. There's lots of bruising all over the poor lad's body."

"From what?"

"My best guess is balls from the pool table."

"Put inside socks?"

"More than likely."

Emma briefly closed her eyes in sympathy for the poor boy. "How does he seem in himself?"

"No idea, he won't talk," Geoff shook his head then looked at his watch. "Anyway, sorry, but I've got to go," and Geoff got his keys out of the pouch attached to his belt and approached the gate.

Emma hurried along the landing until she came to Sean. He was lying in bed, on his back, one arm up over his eyes. She pulled a chair towards his bed and sat down.

"Hi, Sean, how are you feeling?" she asked gently, looking in horror at his bruised arms and face.

Sean shrugged his shoulders.

"It seems you'll be well enough to go back on the wing tomorrow."

Emma sensed stiffening in Sean's body, but he still didn't speak.

"Is that okay with you?"

Emma decided she may as well be talking to a mannequin, for all the response she was getting.

"Who did this to you, Sean? Was it fellow inmates? Officers?"

Resigned to the fact he wouldn't speak, Emma then said, "I've got that book you wanted. The first one in that science fiction series we were talking about. Anyway, I'll leave it here and you can take it with you back to the wing. Perhaps you'll let me know what you think of it when I see you next."

Standing, Emma leaned down and whispering in his ear said, "I know someone has been bullying you, Sean. Was it an officer? Has someone been saying hateful things to you? Let me help you. But I can't if you won't talk to me."

But her entreaties didn't make any difference. In fact they seemed to have made things worse. Sean turned over in bed, putting his back to her and pulled the covers up around him. She stood there for a moment, wondering how she could reach the boy. She touched him on the shoulder, but he flinched and shrugged her hand away, so she left without saying anything else.

Twenty Two

The next day Sean was taken back to the wing, shuffling alongside a prison officer as they walked from the hospital. Once there, the officer unlocked and opened the gate to the wing, but Sean hung back, too frightened to take the next few steps.

"Come on, lad, in you go."

But Sean couldn't move. He looked through the bars of the gate which had a view down the length of the wing and saw the usual hustle and bustle of recreation.

"I haven't got all day, come on," and the officer prodded Sean in the back.

Left with no choice, Sean walked through the gate, heard the clang of it closing and stood waiting for the officer to lock it behind him. He was feeling worse than when he'd first arrived at Reading HMYOI a few weeks ago. Then he hadn't really known what life inside could be like. He'd been protected by his cell-mate and others who were tasked with inducting new inmates. As he looked down the wing, a cluster of prisoners cleared and he could see the pool table at the bottom of the corridor. The two men playing stopped and turned to look at Sean. As they recognised him, a sneer formed on the face of one of the players. He picked up a ball from the table and tossed it from one hand to the other, never taking his eyes off Sean. A burst of laughter defused the tension, but the message wasn't lost on Sean.

He bolted for the stairs, grabbed the handrail and hobbled his way upwards towards his cell. Every footstep was agony. He pulled himself up with bruised arms, his legs trembling as he climbed each step. At the top he had to stop and catch his breath and try and still his shaking body.

"You alright, mate?" someone asked.

Sean kept his head down and nodded.

"Need any help?"

"No," Sean managed to reply and pushing himself off the handrail shuffled to his cell as though he were an old man of 70, not a young one of 17.

"Fucking hell," Matt, his cell mate exclaimed at the sight of him. "I thought you might be a bit roughed up, but Jesus, this is ridiculous."

Sean could feel Matt's eyes on him, no doubt taking in the large bruises on his face and split skin across his nose. Even Sean had to admit he didn't look much like himself. He looked more like the bad guy in an action movie, the one who had just been beaten up by the hero.

"Here," said Matt, "take my bunk. You'll never climb up to yours, not the state you're in."

"Thanks," Sean mumbled through split lips. The kind gesture brought tears to his eyes. Prisoners were very protective of their beds and their possessions. They weren't given up lightly. Sean had to swallow hard. He didn't want to cry in front of anyone, not even Matt.

"Who was it, Sean? Who did this to you?"

Sean sank onto the small bed, shook his head and swung up his legs. Sinking back onto the pillow he closed his eyes and put his arm across them and stayed that way. Matt took the hint and left him alone, pulling the door closed behind him, which gave Sean a modicum of peace and hid him from prying eyes. Sean couldn't tell Matt who had done this to him. One of the first things prisoners learned was that if anything happened to you, or you saw something happening to someone else, you didn't grass to the officers, or even to other inmates. He was as frightened of the bullies thinking he was a grass, as he was of them thinking he was a nonce. Either way spelled bad news for Sean.

He continued to lie on his bunk for the remainder of the day, caught in the clutches of depression, unable to see a way out of his current situation. It was early evening when he swung his legs off the bunk and sat up. He was due to ring his Mum. They had an arrangement. He would call her at least every other day about this time. On the one hand he wanted to ring her, as he was desperate to hear her voice. But on the other he didn't, as she would soon realise there was something wrong with him. Either way he was fucked, so he decided to call her. It was better than dealing with her anger at a missed call, the next time he spoke to her.

Sean hadn't been able to eat much of the sandwiches they'd been served for tea. Chewing was out of the question because of his sore face and jaw and, he'd found out he had loose teeth. So he was the first to the phones, as everyone else was still chomping and chatting in their cells.

"Mum," he managed to mumble as she answered her mobile.

"Oh, Sean, I was hoping it was you. How's things? Everyone is fine here. I've been to see Candice and she's okay as well. She's looking forward to seeing you again."

"Mmm," managed Sean.

"Mind you, her father is still creating a bit of a stink, but she's sure she can talk him round."

Another, "Mmm," was all he could manage.

"Sean? What's the matter?"

"Nothing," he mumbled.

"Yes there is. What's happened? Are you alright?"

"No, not really," he decided he had to tell her something. "I got into a bit of a fight that's all."

"Fight? That's not like you. What were you fighting about?"

"Dunno, they just started on me."

There was no way Sean was about to tell her what the bullies had called him and the reason why they'd beaten him up.

"Are you hurt?"

"Just bruised mostly, don't worry, I'll be fine."

Every word was killing him. Not only because of his injuries, but because he was lying to his mum. He wasn't fine, not at all. Not by any stretch of the imagination. He wanted to go home. He shouldn't be in prison. He hadn't meant to do anything wrong.

He sniffed back tears and said, "Sorry, mum, got to go. I'll ring you tomorrow, okay?"

Before she could reply he replaced the receiver. Leaning his head on the wall next to the phone, he allowed the tears he hadn't been able to shed before, fall unabated. He wasn't sure how much more of this he could take. Thank God his case would be dropped soon. His brief had assured him it would only be a few more weeks. He just hoped he'd be able to get through them.

Wiping his face with the sleeve of his tee-shirt, he stole a glance over his arm. There still wasn't anyone around. With a bit of luck he'd be able to get back to his cell without being seen. He pushed off from the wall and hopped and skipped his way over to the stairs, glancing over his shoulder as he went.

Twenty Three

Janet Smith looked at her mobile after Sean had ended the phone call. What the hell had that been about? She wandered into the kitchen to make herself a coffee, turning the phone over in her hand as she went. She put the phone down, clicked on the kettle and spooned coffee into a mug. The she retrieved her phone, selected contacts and looked up the number for Reading Prison. Shrugging, Janet changed her mind again and replaced the mobile on the counter. She poured hot water onto the coffee granules and grabbed the milk out of the fridge, splashing it into the mug.

Turning to lean against the kitchen work-top, she held the mug in both hands. Sean hadn't sounded himself at all. First of all his voice was strange. It was as though he couldn't get the words out through his lips. Secondly, he said he'd been in a fight. That wasn't like him. He was gentle and kind. A good boy. Not someone who ran with gangs and for whom fighting was normal. She'd never heard of such a thing.

She swapped her mug for her phone. The contact for Reading Prison was still showing, so she pushed the call button before she could change her mind.

"Reading HMYOI," said the operator.

"Um, I'm not sure who I want."

"Alright, tell me why you're phoning and then I'll tell you who you need to speak to."

"Oh, thanks, it's about my son, Sean Smith."

"What wing is he on," the operator interrupted.

"The Remand wing," replied Janet.

"Putting you through," the operator said, leaving Janet with her mouth open as she'd just been about to speak.

"Remand wing," a male voice intoned.

"I'd like to speak to someone about Sean Smith, please," Janet said.

"What about him?"

"Well, he seems to have been in a fight."

"And?"

"And he's injured. Said he'd got into a fight, but he never fights. There's something wrong."

"Very well, I'll try the wing Governor for you."

After what seemed like a very long wait and just as Janet was about to put down the phone, thinking they'd forgotten all about her, a voice said, "wing Governor."

"Oh, thank goodness. I wonder if you can help me."

Janet proceeded to tell him about her son. How he'd been in a fight. How he never fought. How he was injured. How worried she was - until she was interrupted in mid flow.

"Okay, I'll make a note."

"Make a note? What does that mean?"

But Janet was talking to a dead phone. She'd no idea who she'd just spoken to or what, if anything, he intended to do about it.

She put the mobile down and grabbed her coffee. Looking into its murky depths she wished she knew what was going on. Wished she could see through the coffee to the wing where Sean was. She felt so bloody useless.

Gulping down her now lukewarm drink, she put the mug in the sink and headed into the other room. She was going on-line. If she couldn't get anything out of the establishment, surely she could get some helpful information from the internet.

Twenty Four

It was nearing the end of a long day for Emma. She wasn't any further on with finding out what had happened to Sean Smith, nor with her questioning of the prison officers. They had clammed up. She pushed her way into the Admin office to be greeted by Joan.

"Ah, Emma, glad you're back. He wants to see you," and Joan indicated the Governor's office with a pointed finger.

"Oh, bugger. When?"

"Now, if not sooner."

"Shit. Alright, I'll just put these down."

Once she had dropped off her files, she walked to Governor Sharp's office. Tapping on the open door, she said, "You wanted to see me, Governor?"

"Ah, Emma, come in please. Oh, and close the door behind you."

Not a good sign, Emma thought. Not a good sign at all. What on earth did he want? She ran through her current failings, arguments and frustrations, but couldn't come up with anything serious enough to be brought to the Governor's attention.

Once Emma was seated in front of his desk he said,

"It appears you've been talking to the prison officers."

"Yes, Governor, I do that all the time. Is there a specific conversation you want discuss with me?"

She knew she should mind her p's and q's around the Governor, not indulge in sarcasm, but all she wanted to do was to go home and she rather hoped he'd get to the point.

"Specifically," Sharp emphasised the word to the point of mockery, "conversations you've been having about the attitudes of the officers towards those prisoners with mental health problems."

"Ah," said Emma, thinking that she'd get Tom for reporting her. Once her conversation with Tom had come to the Chief's attention, he would have taken great pleasure in passing that knowledge onto the Governor.

"I find it unconscionable that you seem to think the officers, or even one officer, would be so insensitive as to goad young vulnerable prisoners." Both his voice and his eyes were hard, conveying to Emma the message that she was in deep shit.

"But surely it's not outside the realms of possibility, Governor?" Emma asked, having decided she had nothing to gain by keeping quiet, so she may as well try and get something positive out of the conversation.

"What evidence do you have?"

"Well, no hard evidence as such. But that doesn't mean there isn't something going on. I've just got this feeling. Our record on suicides is not an enviable one, I'm only..."

"Trying to help?" interjected the Governor.

"Well, yes."

"Then I'm afraid you're not being helpful at all. You're in danger of stirring up unrest within the officer ranks and endangering the good relations between officers and governors. So, don't let me hear you've been meddling again. Understood?"

"Yes, Governor."

"Off you go then, I'll see you tomorrow."

"Thank you, sir," Emma said and left his office thinking how unfair it was. But at least she'd not apologised. As far as she was concerned, she'd nothing to apologise for and in the meantime, she wanted a word with Tom.

She found him on the Remand wing.

"Tom, could I have a word please?"

"Sure," he said. "Let's walk," so Emma followed him along the wing landing.

"Why did you..."

"Go to Chief Robinson?" he interrupted.

"Exactly, I've just been hauled over the coals by the Governor. I really didn't think you'd do that to me. I thought we were friends."

"Sorry, Emma, it was a knee jerk reaction. After I'd told him, I felt dreadful and since then I've been mulling over your concerns and well, I think you have a point."

"You do?" Emma stopped walking.

"Yes, I can't put my finger on it, but I think there's something not quite right. It's just an atmosphere on the wing. It's not all the time, though, so I'm trying to work out what it could be, or who it could be, that is affecting the lads sometimes."

Emma felt relief flooding her body. "Oh thanks, Tom, I'm glad it's not just me that thinks something is off kilter."

"I'll let you know if I come across anything strange."

"Without going to the Chief first?"

Tom grinned, "Without going to the Chief first," he agreed.

"Cheers. Take a close look at who is on duty at those times, would you? I also want to hear about any lads that have been alright in the past, suddenly becoming withdrawn and sullen. Those who previously enjoyed particular activities but now have no interest in anything."

"The only thing I can think of that changes on the wing, is when we have supply officers in."

"Supply officers?" Emma smiled to herself, but didn't say anything else, wanting to see what Tom thought about them, before voicing her own opinion.

"Yes. Since the cut backs, we have to rely more and more on supply or contract staff. It may be one of them, you never know."

"You never know," she agreed. "Thanks, Tom. I'll look into that as well."

Sean Smith lay on the bottom bunk in his cell, head towards the door, where he'd been for most of recreation. After eating his cardboard sandwiches, his cell mate Matt had gone out to see one of the lads who wanted help writing a letter to his mum. Those prisoners who were better educated tended to help out those less fortunate when they could. The number of illiterate prisoners on their wing alone was frightening. It seemed so many of them had played truant from school and then left full-time compulsory education at the earliest possible opportunity, without even mastering the basics of reading and writing.

Lying on the bunk, Sean couldn't help but overhear the conversation between the assistant governor and the officer. He recognised Emma's voice and that of

Tom Collins, one of the more decent screws on the wing. What he heard didn't fill him with hope that things would get better any time soon. Not only did he have the wing bullies to deal with, but by the sounds of their conversation, bullying officers as well.

He looked up at the underneath of the bunk above him. He felt the pressure of it weighing down on him. He turned over onto his side to find the wall inches from his nose. The cell had never seemed so small. He was trapped in the tiny space, within the confines of the bunk. Above was metal, to one side concrete and the other side bullies that enjoyed the sport of kicking a man when he was down. He was trapped in a space no bigger than a coffin. He began to panic. His pulse raced and he tried to suck air into his lungs, but nothing happened. He breathed faster and shallower, feeling as though he were suffocating, desperate to catch his breath. But it didn't work. His chest heaved, his head began to swim and he thought he was going to die. Die from lack of oxygen. Die from claustrophobia.

Then suddenly Matt was there, pulling him up. Sean looked at Matt bug eyed, unable to speak, unable to tell him what was wrong. Pulling Sean into a seated position, Matt then emptied the paper bag he'd brought back from the canteen.

Bunching up the neck of the bag, he put it over Sean's mouth saying, "It's okay, breath into the bag. You're hyperventilating. Come on, breath. In. Out. In. Out. That's it."

Gradually, Sean managed to get some control and he gave Matt a watery smile of thanks. The whole experience had left him limp and exhausted. At least it was nearly time for lock-up. Once he and Matt were locked in for the night, he would be safe.

Twenty Five

The kettle clicked off as the water reached boiling point and Emma poured it into two mugs, over the coffee granules and the milk. She quickly stirred the coffee and oblivious to the mess she'd made on the work surface, she carried the mugs through to Billy who was in the sitting room.

"But I can't just leave it," she said, carrying on the conversation they'd been in the middle of when she went to make the coffee. "How would I feel if any more lads committed suicide?"

"I'm not saying you should leave it," Billy replied, having personal experience of dealing with the aftermath of the suicide of several soldiers. "It's just that you have to approach it in a different way."

"It's the bloody Governor that's at fault," she said, starting to get angry again. "And bloody Tom. Can you believe it? Dobbing me in like that."

Billy started to laugh.

"What the hell are you laughing at?"

"Dobbing me in! God I haven't heard that term in years, not since school," he was still chuckling.

"Really, Billy is that all you can say? I'm trying to

have a sensible conversation with you about something that is really important to me and all you can do is be flippant."

"Emma,"

"Don't you care about people's lives?" she demanded, her voice rising. "Or are you just as bad as the idiots at the prison; Chief Robinson and his cohorts, including Albright the Head of Operations. They're so busy wiping each other's arses they haven't got time to do their jobs properly."

"Emma, stop it."

"Don't tell me to stop it!" Emma was spluttering with rage, unable to stem the flow of her anger, the hot lava of words spewing out of her mouth. "How dare the Governor tell me to stop making waves and to think about the smooth running of the prison. I don't bloody believe it."

"Emma, shut up!"

She spun round to face him, tears in her eyes. "I thought you were different. I thought you cared about people. But you're just the same as everyone else."

"If you stop getting so emotional and listen to me, you might find that I do care and you might learn something."

"Oh, really," she sneered, "The big Billy Williams telling the angry little girl what to do."

"See, that's exactly your problem, attacking me because I disagreed with you. Now sit down and shut up and listen to me for once."

Billy had that Sgt Major-type voice thing going on. The tone that tended to cut through the crap and make people sit up, shut their mouths and listen. which is precisely what Emma did, but not without protest. She flounced down in the chair opposite him, refusing to sit next to him on the settee and glared her defiance across the space between them.

"You have got to stop being so emotional. Emotive reactions don't get things changed. Don't help you achieve your objective."

"Very well, what's the soldier's way, then? I suppose that's what you're talking about."

He carried on as though she hadn't spoken. "You must step back emotionally and speak to people as colleagues that you respect."

"But I..."

"No buts," he cut her off. "That part is non-negotiable. You have to treat people as you would want to be treated yourself. Talk to them in a normal tone of voice. Ask their opinions and then logically spell out what you would like to do and what those actions would achieve to change or resolve the particular situation."

"Oh," said Emma, beginning to get an inkling of what he was talking about. "So instead of me shouting at Chief Robinson about one of his officers, what would you suggest?"

This time her question was genuine and not a sarcastic reaction, as the red mist in her head was dispersing and she began to think more clearly.

"Explain to him that there is a potential problem, but not to worry, you have a strategy for dealing with it. Everyone wants someone to make a problem go away, especially without them having to do anything about it. Remember, there are no problems, only solutions."

"So the same should work with the Governor?"

"Absolutely. Flatter his ego. Say that this particular problem mustn't be allowed to sully his reputation, nor the reputation of Reading HMYOI and that you are determined that won't happen. It's about making him see that you're on his side, if you like."

"I see," she said. "So less shouting, crying, ranting and raving and more sycophantic strategies."

"Exactly," said Billy with some satisfaction.

"Even though I think he's a wanker."

"Yes," Billy laughed. "But Emma, you can't keep judging people the way you do. It's pure arrogance. He might not fit your picture of what an ideal Governor should be like, but he must be somebody's. He hasn't got where he is by being a useless loser."

"But that's precisely what he is," Emma said. "You've no idea what he's like to work for. Always in cahoots with Chief Robinson and Chad Albright and he cares more about his job than he does about the lads in his care. And that's what they are, Billy. They're in our care. They don't deserve an idiot like him. He's a disgrace."

"Emma?"

"What?" she said, glaring at him, daring him to defy her opinion of Sharp.

"You're doing it again. I rest my case."

As the truth of his words hit home, she reigned in her emotions, slowly smiled at him and then said, "All right, you win."

Twenty Six

The wing briefing was over and the Whisperer couldn't wait to get started. He'd found a new target. It seemed there was a lad who had been badly beaten up and taunted because he'd had sex with an under-age girl. He licked his lips in anticipation. It was still too early to do anything, but he kept his eye on the cell. There hadn't been any sign of the lad throughout recreation, so it appeared he was feeling pretty bad. The Whisperer rubbed his hands together, relishing the thought of fresh pickings. The boy would be feeling a damn sight worse very soon indeed.

The call for lock-up went out and he grinned and traded insults with his fellow officers and some of the lads as he went up the wing closing and locking each door as he passed it. Once that was done, they all retired to the wing office.

"Thank Christ that's over with. It must be time for a brew, everyone want one?" Various shouts and cheers met Tom Collin's offer.

The Whisperer glanced at his watch. 8pm. It was still too early. He'd have to wait until at least 11pm and then some before he could go to work.

The evening dragged on as the Whisperer got on with the mountain of paperwork that accumulated in the wing office during the day. A bloody waste of trees was his opinion of the amount of paper the requests garnered, as he sifted through the various applications and forms the prisoners produced every day. There were so many apps and so few officers that he knew many of the requests would never see the light of day. Or if they did, it was normally too late for whatever action the prisoner had requested. He knew of several times when prisoners had requested a home visit for a funeral due to the death of a relative and the acceptance or rejection had been received by the prisoner a week after the event. He smiled to himself. Such was the lot of a prisoner, he thought as he picked up a particularly badly completed form, crumpled it up and dropped it in the waste paper bin by his feet. He knew that by the end of his shift, the bin would be full.

By 11pm the wing had settled down and the Whisperer volunteered for a walk about, using the fact that he was fed up with sorting paperwork and needed a bit of a break as an excuse. He walked along on his rubber soled shoes, which squeaked as he walked. He always fancied the sound was a bit menacing. His slow, steady footsteps squeaking as he approached each door. He lifted the observation hatch of some of the doors as he went, so that when he got to Sean's cell, opening the hatch wouldn't seem unusual.

Looking sideways through the open door hatch into Sean's cell, he could see the lad turning this way and that in the bottom bunk. There was no sound or movement from the top one, just the lump of a still body, the blanket faintly rising and falling with the boy's breathing. Taking care to keep his face out of view he whispered, "How are you doing, Sean? Been hearing all about you, I have. It seems you're the one who likes kids."

Sean's body stiffened under the sheets and stopped its restless fidgeting.

"Under-age sex is what turns you on, isn't it? The younger the better, eh? Is that what you were fantasising about, as you were writhing in your bed?"

Sean turned his back on the whisperings.

"The thing is there's no place in society for the likes of you. Scum of the earth, you nonces are."

The Whisperer detected movement under the blanket.

"You shouldn't be allowed to walk the streets. You need locking up for the rest of your life, you do."

Sean was shaking now, the blanket rippling like waves breaking on the shore. Great gulps of air could be heard being dragged into his lungs. The Whisperer stood there for a moment, savouring the knowledge that he'd got under the skin of the prisoner. By the sounds of it, he had made Sean cry.

"You'll never be let out, you know. The streets need to be kept clean of garbage like you."

The Whisperer closed the hatch and walked back down the wing. Making sure his shoes squeaked as loudly as possible as he went.

Twenty Seven

Mindful of the Governor's words, and of Billy's attempt at teaching her more effective strategies for dealing with problems, Emma decided to stay away from the prison officers and approach her quandary from another angle. If there were supply officers on the wings, the people who would know about it were in the accounts department. Emma figured the contractors would need their wages paying. No one did the job for free. Thinking about it, no one did the job for the money, either, as prison staff weren't amongst the best paid people in England.

She breezed into the accounts department and asked for Sheila, having already discussed with Joan earlier, who she thought would be the best person to talk to. It turned out Emma was already talking to Sheila. Emma was fascinated by the woman's permanent wave so severe that her hair didn't move when Sheila dipped her head. Not an inch. Dragging her eyes away from the monstrous hairstyle, Emma explained to Sheila that she would like details of the payments made to supply officers. To Emma checking with accounts seemed the best way forward for her and thought it would be a quick and easy task to gather the information. But after Emma's explanation, Sheila didn't seem to share her optimism and was as stiff and unmoving as her hair.

"You want what?" she sniffed, her hands frozen over her keyboard.

"Details of when supply officers were employed by the establishment. Going back, say, three months?"

"And how would I find out that?"

"By checking their payments? Don't you pay their wages?"

Emma wondered if the woman ever relaxed. Sheila was sitting ram rod straight in her chair. She wore a neat sweater and matching cardigan, topped by a painted face and lips which were an alarming shade of red and out of step with her pale coloured foundation.

"That's all very well," said Sheila, "but my computer only lists when the payments were made and the amount and not for what period."

"So?" Emma couldn't drag her eyes from Sheila's hair and those lips. She wondered if the lips had been puffed up by Botox injections. They seemed so big and fat and red that Emma had difficulty concentrating on Sheila's next words.

"So, I'll have to pull out the paperwork," she was saying. "I'll need to find the original requisitions, which will show which contractors were on what wing on what dates."

"So you do have the information then."

"I suppose so." Sheila moved a piece of paper from one side of her desk to the other, for no apparent reason that Emma could see. "I suppose I could find it."

"Good, could I have the information as soon as possible? Please?"

"Why?" Sheila looked down her nose at Emma, making Emma want to smash it.

But instead of resorting to physical violence, Emma took a deep breath and then said, "Because Governor Sharp has tasked me with looking into the use of contract staff and he wants me to report back to him in a couple of days. That means I need the information from you by tomorrow at the latest. Or this afternoon if you could manage it."

"Governor Sharp, you say?"

"Yes."

"Oh, well, I'll see what I can do," sniffed Sheila. "But I'll check with Joan first, mind."

"Please do," said Emma, thankful that she'd prepped Joan in advance. Emma would never have set foot in the accounts department without Joan knowing and without them previously having devised a strategy to get Emma what she wanted. "I look forward to hearing from you. Shortly," she said pointedly.

Twenty Eight

It was the hullaballoo of the morning routines that woke Sean. Officers going from cell to cell, making sure everyone was awake and ready to go down for breakfast. The harsh voices of the officers grated, but he supposed at least those normal voices were better than the one last night. The one that had whispered those vile, horrible insults through the observation hatch.

Matt hadn't even woken up while it was happening. Nor afterwards, as Sean lay crying in his bunk. If he had have done, Sean was sure Matt would have shouted out, told the person to fuck off and leave them alone. He was braver than Sean, who by now was afraid of his own shadow.

"Come on, Sean," Matt said his voice imbibed with enthusiasm, an attitude that Sean couldn't even begin to understand. How could anyone sound happy being locked up in here? Sean wanted to disappear into his blankets, but Matt wasn't having any of it.

"Come on," he said, this time throwing the covers off Sean. "You don't want to get in trouble with the screws, do you? Up you get."

Sean realised Matt meant well and more importantly, that he wouldn't take no for an answer, so he swung his legs out of bed. They were still stiff and sore from the beating, but moving around did actually help, once he got going that was. He ran his fingers through his hair, splashed some water on his face and quickly brushed his teeth, all under the scrutiny of Matt.

"Happy now?" Sean said.

"Very," replied Matt. "Come on, last one to breakfast is a ninny!" and he ran out of the cell to join the throng of lads going down for breakfast.

Dear God, thought Sean, it's like living with a boisterous younger brother. As he stood in the doorway, waiting to join the end of the line, he came face to face with his tormentors.

"Well look who it is," said the one called Col. "The bloody nonce."

Behind them, inmates continued to push their way along the landing.

"Hungry are you? Well eat this!" and a fist was smashed into Sean's face. As he fell to the floor, blood pouring from his mouth and nose, he heard hysterical laughter drifting away along the corridor.

He lay on the floor, wondering what the point was of it all? This was no way to live. He was already too frightened to go to recreation, or to walk around the yard at exercise. He would only go to the showers when there were a lot of lads around, and friendly ones at that. Hoping there was safety in numbers. And now it seemed he couldn't even go down to get something to eat.

His tongue explored his mouth and found a broken bit of tooth that he spat out onto the floor. But broken teeth were insignificant in the mess that was his life at the moment. A far bigger problem was his relationship with Candice. From where he was lying it was all his fault. Everything was his fault. He'd been thinking about it all night. Maybe the bullies were right. Maybe there was something wrong with him. He wondered what would happen when Candice grew up? When she reached the age of 18 or 25? Would he still fancy her then? Or did he really only fancy pubescent girls? He didn't know anymore. No wonder her father wouldn't let Sean anywhere near her. No wonder he wouldn't drop the charges.

Still lying on the floor, Sean closed his eyes, decided to give up thinking and drifted off into blessed oblivion.

That evening, once again Sean plucked up the courage to go to the phones. He was desperately ashamed of himself. Ashamed of his sexual activity with an underage girl and for the disgrace he'd brought on his mother. He wanted to tell her he was sorry and that deep seated need was overriding his fear. He'd been thinking about it all day.

That morning one of the screws had found him lying on his cell floor and they'd taken him, once again, to the hospital wing. This time he had a broken nose, but the doctor said there wasn't much he could do about it and had just put some sort of butterfly plaster across the bridge of his nose. Sean didn't think it would do much good. Still, it went with his broken teeth, he supposed. He was told to put in an 'app' for a request to see the dentist, but to be honest Sean didn't hold out much hope of ever seeing one.

He made it to the phones without seeing 'them' and it seemed his luck was still in, for there was a free telephone. Grabbing the receiver, he inserted his phone card and dialled his mother's number.

"Sean? Thank God, I've been so worried about you. I've..."

But Sean interrupted her. "Mubm, I bont to say soby."

"What?"

"Soby."

"Sean, what on earth's happened now?"

"Doze broke, but mm okay."

Without warning, the receiver was wrenched from his hand and he was hit over the back of the head with it.

"Off you go, nonce."

Sean was paralysed with fear and could hear a tinny, "Sean? Sean?" emitting from the receiver.

"I want to use the phone, so do one!"

Sean obeyed the order, as though it was from a screw, not an inmate and scuttled away, like a mouse running from a cat.

Twenty Nine

Janet Smith had to sit down. Her legs wouldn't hold her up any longer and she dropped into a kitchen chair. She pulled her cigarette packet towards her and shook one out. With trembling hands she lit it and had to take several deep drags before she managed to calm down.

Picking up her mobile and then a piece of paper she had written down a number on, she tried her best to dial it. It took three attempts before the numbers were in the right order and she heard the ringing of a telephone at the other end of the line.

As soon as it was answered she said, "My son's in prison, he keeps being beaten up, I don't know what to do. Can you help me?"

The lady on the other end of the call, who worked for the Offenders Families Helpline said, "Okay, just slow down. Let's start with your name."

"Janet Smith."

"Alright, Janet. Is it okay if I call you Janet?"

"Mmm," she agreed.

"So, Janet, my name is Sue. What is your son's name and which establishment is he in?"

The woman's calm questioning helped Janet get a grip on her emotions and she began to tell Sue that her son was at Reading HMYOI and was being beaten up.

"Can you start at the beginning? Why is he there and what makes you think he is being bullied?"

By the end of their conversation, Janet felt a whole lot better. She now had a strategy for helping Sean and it was one that she could start implementing right away. Sue had promised to ring the prison for her, to tell them she knew about the physical attacks and to ask for help for Sean. Janet felt this was a better way of approaching the prison staff, as Sue could be more professional and less emotional than she could ever be. Also the helpline had a good record of being able to cut through the red tape and speak to the right person. As for herself, she was going to ring the Chaplain and ask him to visit Sean and see if he could arrange for a 'listener'. Apparently, they were trusted inmates who had been trained by the Samaritans and could provide confidential support to 'at risk' prisoners. For that was what Janet feared her son was now, at risk. He was at risk of harming himself, or worse, because of the physical and psychological bullying.

But the best bit of information Sue had given Janet, was that she was entitled to visit her son for 90 minutes a week as a minimum and up to a maximum of seven visits a week, as he was a remand prisoner. So she was going to book a visit, for as soon as humanly possible. Her son was in trouble and she wasn't about to turn her back on him. He needed his mum and she wouldn't let him down.

Thirty

The Whisperer unlocked his front door and threw his keys into the bowl on the small table in the hall. He'd had a good night, a really good night. For not only had he started his new whispering campaign, but he'd just been asked to work at Reading for the next two weeks on the same wing as last night. He couldn't believe his luck. Someone had grabbed a late booking for a holiday, a much needed two week break in the sun, so he'd been asked to cover. He'd tried very hard to be casual when he accepted the offer. He hadn't wanted to seem overly enthusiastic or desperate even. That would never do. He couldn't have anyone suspecting anything. He must be careful and continue to be as boring and nondescript as possible. Someone who was just there, a part of the furniture, not someone who stood out.

Still, it really was the best of news. He'd have that lad Sean in the palm of his hand soon. It wouldn't take long. That type of boy sent off vibrations, small interruptions in the flow of the prison air. When he came across one, it made the hairs on the back of his neck stand up. It was as though their pain was a real thing that changed the molecules in the air around them. It was almost as though they had a different smell to everyone else. Try as they might to make themselves small and insignificant, they were as visible to him as though they had a bull's eye target printed on their backs.

He climbed the stairs to change out of his prison uniform and then he thought he'd have a bowl of soup before bed. It really had been a very satisfactory night. Soon another bad boy would be gone. Society would be just that little bit safer without him. The Whisperer would have done his job well. His goal in life, now, was to get retribution for all those mothers who had been badly hurt and let down by their sons. To get some payback for all the insults hurled, dinners not eaten, bills not paid, money stolen and, possibly the worse of all, for all those times they'd been ignored. For the times when their sons had turned their backs on a mother's love, disappeared out of the front door and never gone back.

He sat down heavily on the bed, unbuttoning his shirt. He wished he could unburden himself, as easily as he could remove his clothes. But he couldn't share his secret with anyone. His work was too important to ever entertain the possibility that he might be stopped. He was doing it for all the mums out there who had been let down by their offspring. He was doing it for Janey. And he wasn't about to let her down like her useless good for nothing junkie son had done.

Thirty One

"Hi Geoff," Emma breezed into Dr. Fox's office. She was determined to be upbeat and positive in her dealings with her co-workers, heeding Billy's advice. She knew a change in her attitude would have to be wrung out of her. Anger as a tool for coping with disappointment was ingrained in her, rightly or wrongly, and she recognised it would take work to curb her temper. She was too much like her father in that respect. The one trait she'd hated about him had seemed to have rubbed off on her.

Geoff updated her on the mental and physical condition of the lads in the hospital wing and then Emma asked, "Are there any more vulnerable lads that I should know about?"

Geoff looked askance. "We've just been through the list," he said.

"I know that, Geoff, but is there anyone else that you've seen lately that could be at risk? Anyone I should be looking out for? Anyone I could help you with?"

Emma was hoping her oblique way of making sure Geoff had done all the paperwork and not missed anyone out, would pay dividends. Also her offer of help should swing it as well.

"No," he said, rubbing his chin and shaking his head, "I don't think so."

"Okay, thanks a lot," said Emma, closing her notebook and she rose from her seat on the other side of Geoff's desk and headed for the door. But there she paused.

"By the way, how's Sean Smith?"

When Geoff didn't reply, she prompted, "You remember, the lad who was beaten up with pool balls in socks."

"Oh, him," Geoff's face coloured and he looked down at the desk, seemingly not able to meet Emma's eyes. "He, um, he had his nose broken yesterday," he admitted.

Emma paused, ran her tongue around her teeth, making a soft clicking sound and then deliberately returned to sit at Geoff's desk.

"Had his nose broken?" she said as calmly as she could.

"Yes, he wouldn't say who did it though."

"No," she said slowly, "I don't suppose he would. So what have you done about him? I don't seem to have received any paperwork. Has he been moved into isolation to get him away from the bullies? Or transferred to onto another wing?"

"Not at the moment, no."

Emma, by now, was trying very hard to keep a grip on her emotions. She was perilously close to giving Fox a mouthful for his obvious failure to do his job properly. What the hell was wrong with the man? She shook her head in despair.

"Look, Geoff, don't you think he needs protection?"

"Yes, I'm sure you're right, he does. It's just that I was very busy yesterday and I, um…"

"Forgot?" prompted Emma.

"It seems he may have fallen through the cracks. We are extremely busy and short-handed at the moment, as you are well aware."

It seemed Geoff's desire to cover his arse had given him some backbone and he straightened in his chair and glared at her. But Emma wasn't giving in quite that easily.

"That's all very well, Geoff, but how would you feel if he was the victim of another, more vicious attack? Or decided to top himself to get away from the bullies? He should have been moved into isolation to get him away from the idiots on the wing and also put on suicide watch."

"I wasn't sure being alone was the best thing for him," Geoff gabbled the only excuse he could seemingly muster. "Not with his mental state. I am sure he is suffering from depression."

Emma was convinced that Geoff was making up excuses as he went along. He'd no idea if the lad was suffering from depression. He hadn't had an interview with him. If he had, there would be paperwork. And there wasn't any.

"I realise that, Geoff, but there is a fine line between whether being kept on the wing or being alone is best for the lad. I believe we've had this discussion before. But I have to say that on balance, this time, stopping the attacks by segregating or moving him is probably worth it, as long as the officers realise that he needs to be checked and checked often." Emma could hear her voice rising and she struggled to moderate it. "I tell you what, Geoff, I'll go and see him this afternoon myself and let you have my recommendations."

She strode out of the office before she could hurl an insult at him along the lines that it seemed she needed to do his job as well as hers.

Thirty Two

"So, how did it go today?" Billy asked from the depths of the fridge where he was clattering about, trying to find a beer.

"A lot better, I think," said Emma, who had already poured her customary glass of wine. "But I nearly had a set-to with Geoff Fox."

"Remind me, Geoff Fox is who?"

"The Medical Officer."

Emma tried not to get annoyed over the fact that Billy had forgotten the names of her colleagues. He was as busy as she was and if she was fair, she didn't remember all the names of the people he worked with.

"Anyway," she said and proceeded to tell Billy what a useless arse the man was over his dealings with Sean Smith. "But I managed to keep my cool," she said rather proudly.

"Great. But that's only the start," he said winking at her and taking a swig from the beer bottle he'd managed to find in the fridge and open.

"Only the start?" Emma eyed him with dismay. He had to be joking. She couldn't believe there was more of this agony to come.

"Yes, this is just the beginning of your maturity as an assistant governor and as a person."

"Which means?"

"You've to stop thinking of people as useless arses!" he laughed.

It was just as well he laughed, had made a joke of it, because Emma's stress level was rising and the last thing she wanted was an argument with Billy. But at the same time, he wasn't her father and shouldn't talk to her in a condescending manner. Pushing away thoughts of her absent father, who had always been more interested in work than in his daughter, she took a sip of her wine, settled back against the kitchen work top and prepared to listen to Billy.

"Go on then," she said.

"Well, you've got to do two things. The first is to stop losing your temper."

Emma eyes widened, but Billy had caught the gesture.

"Just like that. You were very quick to react to what you perceived as a slight against you."

"Yes, well," Emma replied. "You wouldn't like to be criticised either."

"But I wasn't criticising, I was just stating a fact. A fact that we'd already discussed."

"You were?" she was dubious about the validity of that claim.

"Yes and that was a prime example of what you mustn't do. You mustn't react emotionally. Take emotions out of the equation and things will be a lot better for you at work."

"Mmm," she mused. "You said firstly. What's the second thing?"

"You must stop criticising your colleagues."

"Do I?"

"All the bloody time. Come on, Ems, you know you do. The question is - what gives you the right to do that?"

"The fact that I do my job well and can't abide it when others don't do theirs," Emma walked over to the window, looking out at the street which had the occasional street lamp providing patches of light punctuating the darkness.

"But that's your perception. You don't really know what's going on with Geoff Fox, do you? You've no idea of how much work he has. You don't know all about his staffing problems and how they affect him, particularly when dealing with an increasing number of ill inmates. Am I right so far?"

"Well..."

"And how long as Fox been a Medical Officer? Hell, how long has he been a doctor?"

"Quite a few years, I guess," Emma had to concede as she turned away from the window to look back at Billy. "He's in his mid 40's I suppose."

"So he has rather more experience in his field than you do, to be fair."

"Fair!" Emma seized on the word. "What's fair about it, when young lads are killing themselves and senior management don't give a damn?"

She walked across the kitchen into the living area and sank into a chair.

Billy followed her and kept talking. "Look, keeping your cool doesn't mean you don't care. If you're hell bent on exploring the fact that there might be a rogue prison officer behind the suicides and the increasing number of lads who are being put on suicide watch, then you need to be able to investigate without losing control, losing your cool or getting into trouble with the Governor."

"I suppose so."

"Not suppose so, definitely, Emma. It doesn't mean you care less, just that you handle things better, deal with people properly and present your case with facts and with reason. If you change your attitude and be more mature, you will more easily reach your goal."

Emma nodded slowly. Perhaps he had a point. "I'll try."

"Good, so, no more snap judgments or criticism of staff. Okay?"

"Okay," she grumbled and lifted her wine glass to her face, to hide her expression of anger from Billy.

Thirty Three

The next day, Emma had the first test of her new strategy. She did have to admit that Billy was right, albeit grudgingly. She was quick to criticise others and knew she had to make much more of an effort to get on with people. She liked it at Reading and anyway she didn't want to waste the past two years of climbing up the ranks. So easy does it, she breathed as she entered the Remand wing.

She looked, in vain for Sean Smith, so spying his cell mate, Matt, she moved over to ask him where Sean was.

"In the cell, miss," said Matt walking away.

"Okay, I'll go and see him in a minute. Matt?" she called him back.

"Yes, miss?"

"How does Sean seem to you?"

Matt stood and looked at Emma, appearing to have some sort of internal debate as to whether he should talk about his friend to a governor or not. He started to speak, then stopped, then opened his mouth before closing it again. Emma waited. But then Matt said, "Not so good, miss, I'm afraid."

"Do you know who's bullying him?"

Matt dropped his eyes to look at the floor. "No, miss, not really. I never saw them, both times, sorry, miss."

"Okay, look can you keep an eye on him? Let the officers know if he gets worse, self harms, anything like that."

"Yes, miss."

Emma could see Matt was edging away and kept eyeing the pool table, where one of the lads was waiting, two cues in his hands.

"Off you go, play your game of pool. Thanks, Matt."

As the young man rejoined his game, Emma's eyes swept along the wing and rested on a prison officer she hadn't come across before. Wondering who he was, she watched as a lad came running down the recreation area.

"Oy!" the officer boomed. "What the hell do you think you're doing?"

"Sorry, sir," the lad slid to a halt next to the officer.

"I should bloody well think so," the officer retorted. But instead of letting the lad carry on to finish whatever urgent task he was hell bent on, the officer grabbed the lad's arm and began to whisper in his ear.

As Emma walked towards the two of them, she saw the inmate's eyes widen and his face blanch, all the while kept in place by a firm grip on his arm. What the hell was going on? Then the officer shook the boy's arm before pushing him away leaving him to stumble over to his friends.

Emma wanted to go and see if the boy was alright and ask what the officer had whispered in his ear. But she had to be careful not to undermine the authority of the prison officers on the wing. It was a delicate balance between respect and authority and she couldn't be seen to berate an officer in public.

She desperately wanted to go over to him and ask what the hell he thought he was doing, but instead she clenched her fists and curled her toes and left it. But she filed away the incident for future investigation. Thinking about Billy's words of wisdom, she realised that a shouting matching during recreation between a governor and an officer, would mean that not only would she would get into trouble, but she would lose the respect of the officers as well as the inmates. And possibly cause a riot at the same time.

Could he be the one that is taunting the lads? The one they call the Whisperer?

She'd have to talk to Tom.

Thirty Four

"Thank you for seeing me, Governor," Emma said as she sat opposite his desk.

"Yes, well, I hope it's about something constructive, Emma. I do have a lot to get through today," and he looked pointedly at his watch.

Clearly he wasn't going give an inch, so she had to be quick and professional.

"I think I've identified a problem, sir," at his glower, she quickly added, "but I also have possible solutions to the problem."

That seemed to mollify him as he said, "Very well, Emma, spit it out."

"Well, sir, it's about the rising suicide rate."

"There's a surprise."

"Please, sir, I believe I've identified a real threat."

"Go on then," he shook his head and looked at his watch again.

"From talking to some of the lads and a couple of prison officers, there's a feeling that an officer is going around making abusive, hateful comments about the inmates. He's goading them, trying to break down their self esteem. It's a horrible form of bullying and we need to stop it."

"And this has come from some of the lads?"

"Yes, sir, and completely unrelated boys, at different times and from different wings."

"This is going to be very difficult to prove, if it's true."

"I do believe it is true, Governor. Why would anyone make up a story like that? It's badly affecting moral, especially that of the more vulnerable."

"As I said, difficult to prove. You can't go around accusing prison officers of something when all you have is a bad feeling and some rumours."

"I have a couple of ideas about that, sir. From discussions with some of the officers," Emma hoped her exaggeration wouldn't be found out, as she'd only spoken to Tom, "it is possible it's a supply officer. I've tried to get evidence of this, but unfortunately I'm being obstructed by the Accounts Department."

"Explain."

So Emma did. She also talked about how an increase in suicides would look bad on the establishment and on the administration.

"In 2009 an investigation into a suicide here at Reading criticised prison staff and recommended the governor and deputy governor be subjected to a disciplinary investigation after it emerged that some night custody officers had slept or watched television while the inmate who also had a history of self-harming, took his own life, after several attempts, with a makeshift ligature. Night-custody officers should have monitored the 17 year old in his cell every 15 minutes. However his body was not discovered until around 40 minutes after his death."

The Governor blanched at the part about

disciplinary investigations, as Emma had hoped he would. Pressing home her point she said, "That can't happen again and as there is a lot of self harming and suicidal thoughts around at the moment, I thought I would have a word with the officers. Perhaps if I could ask them to come in 30 minutes early for their shift?"

After a pause, Sharpe nodded and said, "Very well, organise that with Chief Robinson and as for Accounts..."

"Yes, Governor?"

"Tell them I want the information about supply officers by the end of the week. Thank you, Emma that will be all."

Emma opened her mouth to protest at the lead time given to the Accounts department. It was only Monday, which meant another five days of waiting, another five days of potentially damaging whispers for the lads. But she remembered Billy's warnings and instead of expressing her opinion in the most derogatory terms she could think of, she mumbled, "Thank you, Governor," and left his office.

While she was still in a grovelling mood, just, Emma decided to find Chief Robinson next. She managed to catch him in his office, which was immaculate as usual. Emma managed to work with stuff strewn everywhere, but not Chief Robinson. There was one file on his desk, clearly the one he was working on, as it was open. The only other objects on the desk were his computer monitor and keyboard and a tub of pens and pencils. Emma eyed the workspace with some jealousy, wishing her office and desk looked as conducive to work as this. Perhaps that might be something she could aspire to in the future? But for now, she was concentrating on being nice to people enemies.

"Chief, a quick word?" she asked from the door and walked in without being asked.

"Yes, Miss Harrison," his clipped sharp words matching his immaculate hair and uniform.

Emma decided to plunge right in. "I've just come from the Governor," she paused for dramatic effect, which was completely ignored. "He's agreed I could talk to the prison officers." The Chief raised an eyebrow. "Talk to them about the ways of treating vulnerable prisoners and the policies and procedures. It's just a refresher, really, in response to the recent spate of suicides and increased numbers of those who are self harming." Emma decided to keep the rumours of the Whisperer to herself.

"Very well," he sighed with exaggeration. "But I have no idea when I could fit it in."

"There's no need, Chief, I was hoping people might come in say 30 minutes early for their shift."

"That's probably the best, time wise." He peered at her and she managed to stop looking as though she were pleading with him, returning his gaze with a cool stare. "Okay, I'll organise it, on two conditions. One, that I'll be there and the other is that attendance will be voluntary, not mandatory."

"Fair enough," Emma agreed. Let's face it she had no choice but to, she realised. "I appreciate this, Chief."

"I'll let you have the times and dates later on today, because we'll need two sessions, one for day staff and one for night staff," and he then pointedly turned to look at his computer monitor, effectively dismissing her.

Emma left his office thinking that perhaps there was something to this more measured way of dealing with people after all.

Thirty Five

Chief Robinson was as good as his word and a couple of days later, Emma was standing facing the officers who had agreed to come to her morning briefing. As she waited for any stragglers to arrive, Emma watched those already there. Most were studying the notice boards. One board contained photographs identifying their most dangerous inmates. Another reminded staff of items they mustn't bring with them to work which ranged from wax, chewing gum, magnets and Blu-Tac, to memory sticks, mobile phones and metal cutlery.

There was also information notices everywhere, reminding staff of the prison's core values, juxtaposed with a summary of the past week's security incidents. These covered threats on staff, assaults on staff, drugs related incidents, weapons recovered and occasions of bullying. Interestingly enough, she saw that threats against staff and threats against inmates were pretty much on a par. One encouraged staff to speak to management if they were concerned that any member of staff or an inmate could be involved in corrupt or unethical practices.

Once the room settled down, Emma expressed her

gratitude as she welcomed them. She started with her objective, which was to discuss the ways of identifying and treating vulnerable prisoners.

"But what I really want," she said, "is your take on things. What is your attitude to this type of prisoner and what do you think can be done, or should be done?"

"Our personal attitude or the company line?" a male officer asked.

Emma smiled, "Your personal thoughts would be appreciated. This meeting isn't being recorded and no one will hold against you any views you express here. I just want a debate, so we can perhaps enlighten and inform each other. For instance, far more attention is being paid to mental health problems, as we realise how many inmates are arriving with serious issues. A third of the prison population are on the mental health team's books, a large number are taking drugs for ADHD and depression. A significant number have a low IQ and very high levels of anxiety. This in turn is leading to a rise in incidents of self harm."

"That's all very well," said a young female officer. "But we, as officers on the front line, are rarely included in self harm monitoring reviews."

"And you think you should be?"

"Definitely. Obviously not every officer, but say one nominated officer from each wing should be there, so that officer can then draw to our attention any problems with particular lads."

"Excellent," said Emma, scribbling, as there was a murmur of agreement from others in the room. "So you think their background is a factor of their behaviour?" she asked the meeting in general.

"Suppose so," an older male officer said, rather grudgingly Emma felt.

"Of course it is," offered another.

"That's as may be," the older man said. "But the inmates put themselves here in the first place. Their background isn't an officer's fault, nor an officer's problem. All that matters is their behaviour while they're here."

"But there's a direct correlation between the two," insisted another.

"Maybe there is," the original speaker said. "But it still doesn't change the fact that we have to deal with their difficult behaviour on a day to day basis. To me it's irrelevant why they behave as they do. We have to manage the fall out."

"Don't you have any sympathy for them?" a younger female said.

"No. But that doesn't mean I can't treat them fairly and within the rules. Being some sort of bloody social worker or chaplain isn't part of our job specification."

"The other thing I wanted to debate," Emma decided to try and defuse tension the current conversation was causing, "is answering calls from the cells. We were criticised in the last official review for taking too long to respond to them. Has this improved do you think?"

"Are you for real?"

Emma looked towards the back of the room at a different speaker, a middle aged black officer.

"I'm sorry?"

"Don't you realise that's just what the lads do? They bash their doors, just for the hell of it. If we responded to every shout, bang and call we'd never get anything done."

"So how do you decide who to respond to?"

"We have to check on the most vulnerable,

obviously. But we can only do that if there are enough of us on the wing and if we haven't had some other inmate kick off, which has taken most of the officers on shift to respond that an incident. Doesn't anyone realise that we try our best? Why are we always blamed instead of being praised for doing a bloody hard job?"

Having worked as a prison officer during her training, Emma did have some sympathy with the man's views.

"I totally get what you're staying, but in the case of the most vulnerable lads, their background has moulded them into who they are and they need help, not judgment and understanding not hatred."

"Aye and we need understanding not hatred too!"

Emma was glad of the good natured chuckling that broke out. She was also aware that she was in danger of getting on her hobby horse, which would alienate the men and women in front of her, who did a very hard and very dangerous job.

"In summary, then, if we could get one officer on each wing to attend the self harm monitoring reviews and report back to the others, then there would be a greater understanding of those lads who are particularly vulnerable. That would then inform officer's decisions as to which calls to answer quickly, over other calls, which are usually just for attention. Yes?"

Her question was met with nods of approval, so Emma thanked them for their time and wrapped up the meeting. Breathing a sigh of relief that the ordeal was over, as the officers filed out of the room, Emma saw Chief Robinson watching her. Then he smiled, nodded and left the room. Praise indeed from the dour Chief Prison Officer.

Thirty Six

Emma and the Chaplin were winding up their meeting about vulnerable inmates and their conversation turned to Sean.

"I spoke to his mother yesterday," said Father Batty. "She's very upset about the change in Sean's demeanour; she says she's never seen him like this."

"I doubt he's ever been like this," replied Emma. "He was picked up by the police without any warning, thrown in jail and is now being bullied. His world has literally been turned upside down."

"She's also been in touch with the Families Helpline."

"That's right it's why I've become involved in his case. I should have had the paperwork through the proper channels, but," Emma shrugged her shoulders, for once unwilling to heap abuse on those not doing their jobs properly. She was beginning to see that being angry was just a waste of emotional energy, which left her drained and depressed and she was learning to keep a lid on her emotions. Just.

"Let's hope it makes a difference to him," the Chaplin said.

"Well, it should do. Now we have a professional multi-pronged approach we will be able to support him better. You can help with the spiritual side, there's a listener in place to support him from an inmate point of view. Dr Fox is finally in the loop as is the Mental Health team. We're still awaiting an appointment for him with them, but at least he's in the system now. I've made it clear to everyone that he's a high risk possible self-harmer or even capable of an attempt at suicide. That's the last thing I want to happen, another boy dying." Emma closed her files and looked down at her hands.

"And how are you?" Father Batty asked.

"Me?" she looked up at him. His benign face reminding her of a father figure, which of course, was one of his roles within the establishment.

"Yes. You work so hard on behalf of the inmates. I just wondered how you were coping with the stress?"

"Oh, you know." Emma found herself blinking away tears, as she was sideswiped by a rush of emotion But she couldn't cry, she admonished herself. It wouldn't help any of her lads and it wouldn't help herself. She couldn't turn into a blubbering wreck over pressure of work. She had to be stronger than that for goodness sake.

"Really," Emma sniffed, "I'm fine." She swallowed and stood up. "Thanks for everything, Father," and she left the office before he could say anything else that would touch a nerve.

Upon her return to her office, Joan handed her a report. "I think you better get a cup of coffee and make sure you're sitting down before you read this," she said.

"What on earth is it?" Emma pulled her glasses off the top of her head and read the cover page.

"The report into the death of Connor Reece," said Joan.

"That bad?" asked Emma.

Joan nodded her head, so Emma took her advice and it was with some trepidation that she opened the report, with a coffee at her elbow and her door firmly shut.

Thirty Seven

Joan was right. The report was pretty damning in its conclusions.

Connor clearly was a vulnerable young man whose youth worker identified that he would not be able to cope with prison. He was recognised as a suicide risk by Court custody staff and was remanded to HMYOI Reading with a suicide/self harm warning form. However, this form was not received by the induction team, and as a result of this no F2052SH (Self Harm Risk Assessment Order) was opened during his induction period.

During the first two months in Reading HMYOI Connor was found in his cell with a ligature on four occasions and once following a failed self harm attempt. Inexplicably a F2052SH was still not raised. The following week, Connor was found in his cell one morning, bleeding to death from several wounds. Despite the heroic attempts of a member of staff, it was not possible to resuscitate him.

Upon hearing the evidence, the jury identified the following factors as relevant to the circumstances of Connor's death:

1. The failure to open a F2052SH, following a recommendation to do so by Connor's social worker. Instead prison staff recorded that Connor would be assessed by healthcare. There is no documentary evidence that such an assessment took place.

2. There was a lack of evidence to show that the concerns raised by a YOT worker about Connor's history of depression and self harm risk at the time of his incarceration, were recorded by Court custody staff.

3. The lack of documentary evidence that a cell sharing risk assessment review took place following Connor's request to share a cell, the day after the death of another vulnerable young man at the establishment.

4. The failure to undertake an overall review of all documentation relating to the management of Connor, as a result of which potentially significant events were overlooked.

Emma brushed away the tears that had run unchecked down her face as she read the report. In her mind she saw once again the awful sight of Connor in his cell. She smelled again the coppery stench of blood. Felt his dead chest under her hands as she tried to resuscitate him with CPR.

The report made very grim reading. But even more depressing was the question - how far had they come since then, if at all? Time and time again it seemed to Emma that failure to follow protocol, all along the line, meant that boys like Connor were a tragedy just waiting to happen. The weight of responsibility sat on her shoulders and she wondered if she was strong enough to endure the Herculean trials she knew were ahead of her. She was beginning to wonder if she should make a point of checking the background and needs of each young man that entered the establishment. After a gulp of coffee Emma realised that would be a hopeless task. She would never get anything else done if she tried to do everyone's jobs for them.

Reading through the points once again, it seemed that the failure wasn't just at the point of entry. Despite the gaps in the information presented to the establishment when Connor arrived, induction staff had done their job well. They'd made the correct recommendations that Connor should be formally assessed by the Healthcare Team. The failure really came in the decision not to order a Self Harm Risk Assessment Order. Around the same time, Connor had been moved to another wing, which meant the officers on the new wing had no idea that Connor was at risk. However, it did seem that Connor himself had realised how depressed and vulnerable he was, by requesting to be moved to a double cell so he would no longer be on his own. But that request had been either ignored or lost.

Emma hoped the Governor would now put in place procedures to stop it happening again. Which was all very well, she realised. For such procedures would actually have to be adhered if they were to make a difference. Emma wasn't at all sure that would be the case.

Emma had just closed the folder and was leaning back in her chair, eyes closed, when the ringing of her telephone brought her back to the present. It was Sean Smith's mother. She must have been given Emma's name, more than likely by the Families Helpline staff. At least she had good news to report and she told Mrs Smith about the help that had been put in place to support Sean.

"Thank you so much, Miss Harrison," Janet Harrison effused. "You don't know how much it means to me to know that Sean is alright and is being looked after."

Emma smiled to herself. Only a mother would think that an inmate should be looked after like a child. But that's what a lot of the lads in Reading were; children in men's bodies. They had the physical stature but not the emotional maturity to go with it. Sometimes it seemed they were like children in a playground, squabbling about who could play with a particular toy, or take a turn on the slide. Emma was still thinking about that when Mrs Smith said, "You won't let anything happen to him, will you?"

"Of course not," replied Emma. "We're all working very hard to keep him happy and safe."

"Promise me nothing will happen?"

"I promise," said Emma, the two words coming out of her mouth before she was conscious of the significance of them.

Thirty Eight

Emma watched the water swirl into the kitchen sink and the bubbles from the washing up liquid rise up, covering the plates she'd just put in there. She was studying the sink as she couldn't look at Billy after her confession.

"You did what?" he said.

Emma sighed. Billy had reacted exactly as she thought he would. And she couldn't blame him. "I promised Mrs Smith I'd keep Sean safe," she whispered, as though afraid to say the words out loud.

"Jesus, Emma, what the hell were you thinking? How could you say that?"

"Well, it just slipped out. I meant it at the time. It was only later that I understood the implication of what I'd said."

Billy put down the plate he was drying. "Oh, love, you can't go around making promises you can't keep. Think of the emotional damage to Mrs Smith, if anything does happen to Sean. Don't forget it's up to the individual to decide to commit suicide. Sometimes there is nothing anyone can do to prevent it, even though you've tried your best."

"Well, I suppose that's a fair enough assessment," Emma rinsed out the glasses. "But only if an inmate takes his own life of his own free will and not because he's goaded into it."

Emma scrubbed away at the dirty dishes, wishing it was as easy to get the filth out of the establishment as it was to wash crusty pans.

"Whatever do you mean?"

Emma finished with the pan, put it on the drainer and turned to Billy and told him that she thought the officer they called the Whisperer was targeting Sean. The one provoking the inmates by telling them they were no good, good for nothing, a waste of space and that they'd be doing everyone a favour by killing themselves.

"Dear God, you can't be serious? I know you've mentioned him before. You think there really is someone doing that?" Billy wiped down the damp kitchen work surface with his tea-towel. "How are you going to stop him?"

"Well, we know he's been getting at Sean, so we're supporting the boy in every way possible and he's on 15 minute suicide watch. As to stopping the officer, I'm still waiting for the paperwork on the supply officers and I'm going to start visiting the wing at night, or at least after the start of the night shift, when some of them are on duty. I'm also trying to get information out of the lads. He has to be stopped, Billy."

"Be careful," he warned, putting the damp towel over the back of a chair. "Don't make your interest too obvious. I don't want you getting into trouble, or into a potentially dangerous situation."

"I've survived this long in prison, I'm sure I'm okay for a few more years yet," she said.

Thirty Nine

Emma was working late, which was fine. She'd never minded hard work and her drive and professionalism demanded that she do the best she could at all times, even if the work involved filling out numerous forms, which was boring and repetitive. But her paperwork was important. The completion and passing on of forms meant that inmates would get what they needed. This could be anything from requests from prisoners, to recommendations from the health care professionals, to putting support in place for those about to be released. So Emma's paperwork was not just a matter of ticking boxes and filing the reports away, it was about important information that could have a profound effect on an inmate's welfare.

She was just scanning the last file when her phone rang. She put out her hand and answered it absently.

"Emma Harrison."

"Hi Emma, Tom here."

But it didn't sound like Tom, it sounded like someone hissing into the phone.

"Tom? Is that you?"

"Yes. Can you come down to the Remand wing?"

"I guess so. Why?"

"There's someone I want you to see."

"An officer?" Emma sat up straight in her chair.

"Yes," he said and put down the phone.

Emma looked around her office, trying to compose herself, trying to stop the butterflies building in her stomach. She needed to be as professional as she could be, she decided, as she put away her paperwork. This wasn't about escapades and enthusiasm. Realising she needed an excuse to go on the wing, she grabbed the files she had been working on. She had planned to take them down in the morning, so they were an ideal reason for her presence.

She clipped her way along the corridors, stopping and starting at each gate. Her movements were fluid and well practiced, akin to some sort of dance routine. It was a bit like driving down a road at a measured speed so you hit all the traffic lights at green. Rushing in between gates didn't help as Emma then tended to fumble at the locks and lose the time she'd gained by hurrying.

Walking onto the wing she saw Tom in the control office and she strolled in, files in her arms. The other two officers in there nodded a greeting, no one paying her any particular attention, as her presence with piles of files was a normal occurrence. Through the large control room windows Emma had a 180 degree view of the wing. It was approaching 8pm lock-up and the lads were straggling back into their cells.

She approached Tom, with a smile. "Here's the latest lot of apps replied to," she said, passing him the files.

"Thanks," he said. "That should keep some of them happy at least," and he turned away from her to look out of the window.

"Do you need to speak to Sean?" he asked. "Only he's just gone into his cell. Look, first floor landing," Tom pointed. "Just about where Officer Toady is. See?"

Getting his message, Emma smiled. "Yes, thanks, I see him. Why do you call him Officer Toady?" she asked as the other two officers left the control room to herd the last of the lads from association back to their cells. There was a great deal of shouting and cat calling, voices echoing around the vast space, bouncing back down towards the control room. It was as though the noise rang off all the metal on the wing; metal doors, walkways, railings, pipes, gates, keys. The list was as endless as the noise. Even lock-up wouldn't stop all of it, as calls would be made from cell to cell through the windows. Sometimes the shouts were messages, or even threats, but mostly complaints.

"Bad joke I know," said Tom over the din. "It's because of his skin. He has these brown spots on his face. Some of them have growth things hanging from them. It's just a bit off putting to look at."

"What's his real name?"

"Dennis Budd."

"Thanks for that, Tom," Emma said and turned to watch the officer called Budd as he walked along the wing. His gait was nonchalant as he moved from cell to cell, closing and locking the cell doors as he went. From where Emma was standing, she couldn't see if he said anything to the lads as he performed his task.

One by one the officers returned to the control room from their duty on the landings and Emma gathered up her things. She couldn't be seen to be staying too long and anyway she should really have left the establishment a couple of hours ago, as she wasn't on the Duty Governor rota that evening. As she got to the door to leave, she said to the assembled officers, "Oh, by the way, who locked Sean Smith in tonight?" although she knew full well who it was.

"That would be me, Miss..." Toady Budd as Emma thought of him, said. His questioning tone seemed to be asking who the hell she thought she was.

"Sorry, I'm Miss Harrison," she replied, studying him, "Assistant Governor for Inmate Welfare."

Budd said nothing, just looked back at her, a blank expression on his face. He stood quite still. He wasn't glaring at her, but his stare was unnerving all the same.

"How did he seem?"

"How should he seem?" Budd fired a question back at her.

"Sean is one of our more vulnerable inmates," Emma explained. "Everyone is keeping a close eye on him, so I wondered if he was agitated or upset when you locked his door."

"Not that I noticed, miss."

Again that blank stare from Budd. It was most disconcerting.

"Thank you," she managed to say and walked away towards the gate. Glad that she could leave the wing and didn't have to work with the peculiar man who may, or may not, be the Whisperer.

Forty

Tom rang again, early the following morning. He was on his way home and ringing from his mobile phone in the car park.

"Emma, I thought you should know, Sean was a bit of a mess this morning when I opened his cell door."

"Has he hurt himself?"

"No, not that I could see, but he was crying, well, sobbing really. I found his cell mate, Matt, comforting him."

"Oh God, what had caused it do you think? Missing home? His girlfriend?"

"No. He told us that he'd heard whisperings in the night. Someone had been calling him names, telling him that he was no good and that he was a nonce that should be segregated with the other paedophiles. Because that's what he is, nothing more than a kiddie fiddler. But Sean couldn't be sure if it was real or a dream. Poor kid is really messed up."

"I don't suppose he could identify the officer?"

"No, sorry, but well, as you know Toady was on last night...."

"Alright, thanks for the heads up, Tom, I'll see what

I can do to help him."

Emma shivered as she put down the phone. Had Budd been responsible for Sean's distress? At least now she knew that one of the officers that night had been whispering vile insults, but that could be anyone of at least 12 officers, including Tom and Dennis Budd.

Emma knew that a trusted listener from the wing had been helping Sean, so she went off to find him and they managed to have a private conversation in his cell, with Emma standing in the doorway. At first he point blank refused to say anything at all about his discussions with Sean.

"Sorry, miss, but anything the lads say is confidential, you know that. If it isn't, then the system just won't work."

"I know, but can't you see these are exceptional circumstances?"

"Yes, but that still doesn't mean I'll talk."

"Okay, how about trying to answer some indirect questions?"

The listener nodded his agreement.

"Right, has anyone ever spoken to you at any time about a screw victimising them?"

"You've got to be having a laugh, miss. That happens every day on every wing in every prison in England."

Emma smiled wryly, "Point taken. But has anyone talked about a screw in particular, one that whispers in the night?"

She got a reluctant nod to that one.

"One that whispers vile insults, as though he's intent on making the lads feel as awful as possible?"

"Put it this way, miss, there are times when the atmosphere on the wing isn't good. Everyone is on edge. Some of the lads are in bits. And then..."

"Then?"

"Then the atmosphere seems to lift for a bit, go back to normal. But there doesn't seem to be any pattern to it. It that what you wanted to know?"

"That's good enough, thanks a lot."

"And you're trying to do something about it?"

"Yes. This can't be allowed to go on. I'm determined to find out who is doing this."

"Amen to that," the lad agreed.

That evening, Emma had just reached her car when her mobile rang. The display said it was a private number, but Emma decided to take the call, as sometimes her mum rang on Skype and that's how the call came up on the display.

"Yes?" she said, not taking much notice as she was also scrabbling in her handbag for her keys.

"Miss Harrison?" Emma had to strain to hear the words.

"Yes? Who is this?"

"Shall we say a colleague?"

There was something in the voice that stopped Emma. She put her handbag on the roof of her mini and clutched the phone to her ear so she could hear better. "What do you want?" she asked, although she was beginning to get an inkling of who was calling her.

"I can't have you interfering in my work," the voice said. "If you don't stop meddling in things that are none of your business... well let's just say life could get very difficult for you."

The voice was definitely male and mellow, Emma decided and the words seemed to be spoken without emotion. There was no inflection in his speech, which had the effect of making them seem all the more chilling.

"I'm sure you don't want to be reported to the Governor," he whispered.

"Are you threatening me? What would you report me for? I've done nothing wrong. It's you that's in the wrong." Emma was trying not to be affected by the voice, but it was unnerving, hypnotic.

"I'm sure I can find something to report you for, Miss Harrison. You have a nasty habit of getting annoyed with people, shouting, being derogatory. Believe me I've observed several instances of that type of behaviour that I could cite. I've got each incident written down with full details, times, locations, personnel. I'm sure you get the idea."

A shiver ran down Emma's back. But sweat was building on her brow. She realised she was scared. Not of the threats, per se, but by the voice. She wanted him to shut up, to stop.

"Listen you piece of shit," Emma said reacting in exactly the way he had just described her worst type of behaviour. "You leave my lads alone, do you hear? I'm going to catch you, one way or the other."

"But will you be quick enough? Will you catch me before another boy takes his life? Before I rid the prison of one more piece of filth? That's the question, isn't it, Emma?"

Before she could reply, the phone went dead. Emma looked at it in the gloom that was gathering, as the street lamps flickered into life. The most disturbing thing was the way he said her name, caressingly, in that low whisper. She realised her hands were shaking and she was on the verge of tears. All she wanted to do was to get back home to Billy.

Forty One

The next morning, Emma called in on Sean. He was sat on his bunk, looking at his hands.

"Morning," she said, as she poked her head around the door. "How are you today?"

Sean didn't look up, just continued staring blankly at his hands.

"Sean?" she asked gently.

He finally looked up, but she could tell he didn't really see her. There was a faraway look in his eyes as though he were seeing someone or something else. Something inside his head.

"Yes, miss?" he managed, the words drawn out of him like trying to inch out a reluctant cork from a wine bottle.

"Has a listener been to see you? Another prisoner who you can talk your problems through with?"

He nodded and went back to studying his hands, his shoulders hunched, head down.

"Did it help, Sean?"

After a pause, she tried again.

"Would you like another visit? What about your mum? Has she been in to see you?"

To that question Sean managed a slight nod of his head, then started to say something, but in a voice that was so quiet, she had to go into the cell to hear him.

She crouched down in front of him and heard him say, "It's a screw. He whispers vile, evil things in the middle of the night. Is it real or is it a dream, miss?"

He looked up at her, the blank look gone for a fleeting moment. In his face she saw terror and bewilderment.

"I don't understand," he said. "What's happening to me?"

"Oh, Sean, I'm afraid it's not a dream, it's real. But I'm doing all I can to find out who it is and stop him. Have you any idea who it might be?"

But it seemed that their short conversation was too much for Sean. He shook his head, then he began to sob, fell sideways onto his bunk and curled up into a foetal position. Emma stroked his arm for a moment then left him in peace, more determined than ever to do something to stop the evil man.

As she walked along the landing, she slowed as she heard footsteps behind her, the squeaking of a shoe against the floor piercing through the general racket. Turning she saw a figure outside Sean's cell, dressed in a prison officer's uniform. As he disappeared inside, she walked back up the landing, for some reason she couldn't quite place, shivers running through her. As she approached, she stopped just outside the door, standing out of sight of anyone inside. She dropped her eyes to the paperwork in her arms, a ruse, but not a very good one.

"Come on, get up," Emma heard the male officer shout. "Oy, didn't you hear me? Get out of that bloody bunk before I drag you out."

Emma knew that Sean had to be coaxed out of his cell to go and get his breakfast. That way the staff could see him, it would get him out of the cell even for a little while and would also make sure that at least he had the opportunity to eat, even if he didn't actually consume the food. But that wasn't what Emma would call coaxing Sean to get up.

"Listen.... piece of shit... tell you twice," was all Emma could hear of the harsh words the officer was flinging at Sean. Needing to identify him, Emma started to speak to Sean's cell mate, Matt, as he passed her. Chatting nonsense, despite the strange looks from Matt, Emma was eventually rewarded with a look at the officer leaving Sean's cell. What she saw rooted her to the spot. It was Tom.

Quickly turning her back on him, she said to Matt, "Go now, see to Sean, he's in a bad way this morning."

"Yes, miss," said Matt and he dodged into his cell to see to his friend, leaving Emma to look at the retreating back of her own friend, Tom Collins.

What the hell had all that been about, she wondered. He was the last person she would have expected to talk to Sean like that. Was he the Whisperer? Was the story about a supply officer, just that, a story? A hoax to deflect the spotlight away from him and onto another officer? To blame Dennis Budd when it was actually Tom that was the Whisperer?

As she walked back to her office, she pondered the problem. She knew that prison staff were only human, were over stretched and often unable to cope. But was that any excuse for the casual, callous manner Tom had used when speaking to Sean? It was always difficult to deal with a prisoner in crises, having to decide if they had a real problem, or were just weak, or attention seeking cry babies.

But she'd worked with Tom. She couldn't believe he had that sort of attitude to damaged young people. He certainly hadn't in the past. But did he now?

Forty Two

"Hi Emma," came the voice of Phil Goodman who was the Duty Governor that night. He'd just rung her mobile. She turned down the television and concentrated on her phone call. To receive a call from the prison, late at night, she knew something must be wrong.

"What is it Phil?"

"I just wanted to keep you informed. Sean Smith is in a terrible state tonight."

"What sort of state?"

"Nearly catatonic, I'd say. He's just lying there on his bunk, crying. We've been unable to get through to him, neither has his cell mate, Matt."

"What on earth has caused that? I knew he was bad, but not that bad."

"It seems he had a visit from his solicitor late this afternoon. Apparently, his girlfriend's father is still refusing to drop the charges. His case of having sex with a minor is going ahead. It seems it's a terrible blow. Matt told me Sean was convinced her father would drop the charges and all this would go away and he could go home."

"Can you move him?"

"Emma, I've not really got the manpower to do a late night move. It's not a medical emergency as such."

"Not yet it's not."

"No, not yet," Phil had to agree.

"In that case make sure he's watched every 15 minutes would you? He could definitely be a suicide risk."

"Even though he's not alone in his cell? Matt says he'll keep watch."

"Matt can't stay awake all night, as you very well know. Please, Phil, get him checked every 15 minutes. Yes?"

"Yes. Don't worry, Emma, we'll take good care of him."

"Thanks," she sighed and put down the phone, not sure that she'd get a wink of sleep that night, worrying over Sean Smith and his problems that must now seem insurmountable to him. Not only had he to contend with the Whisperer, the man that she still hadn't managed to identify, but now this. He was facing a very serious charge, just because he fell in love with a 15 year old girl.

The sort of news that Sean had received, was one of the root causes of self harm and suicide in prisons. Relationship break-downs were high up on the list of reasons for suicide as well. Other causes were the death of a family member and overwhelming guilt over their crime. Bad news could affect even those who didn't actually present with mental illness at the time of their incarceration, but developed it whilst in prison.

As a result, Emma was still awake when her phone rang once more, a few hours later. Looking at the caller display, it was Reading Prison. Dear God, no, she prayed silently before answering the call.

"Emma, it's Phil again."

"Yes? What's happened? Is he okay?"

"Well, yes and no. We found him trying to hang himself in his cell. Thank goodness you insisted on 15 minute checks."

"Oh my God, how is he now?"

"Well, obviously we got the doctor over and he's now been transferred to the Hospital wing. He's been given something or other, that I can't remember the name of, that should keep him asleep for a few hours. Dr Fox and someone from the mental health team will see him in the morning."

"I will as well, obviously. Thanks a lot, Phil. Thanks to your good work, this time a suicide has been averted."

"But he'll have a long climb back to mental health."

"I know, but at least now he'll have a chance."

Emma put the phone down and leaned back against the pillows. However, her sadness at Sean's condition was pierced with a ray of hope, for once the regime had worked in the boy's favour. She now had to make sure he made it back to at least something resembling the boy he once was. She was well aware that whilst individual officers and some staff may be supportive and good listeners, the Prison Service as a whole was not well equipped to deal with these personal tragedies and crises.

Forty Three

Emma was relieved to find Sean sitting up in bed the next morning. He wasn't exactly bright and breezy, but was at least looking at his surroundings and watching the nurse and doctor as they completed their morning rounds. Anything was better than the catatonic state he had been in last night.

"Morning, Sean."

"Morning, miss," Sean turned his head to look at her. His skin was so pale it was almost translucent and there were black and blue smudges under eyes that were still dull, but at least they were focused on her.

"Can you tell me about last night?" she asked as she sat next to his bed.

"My brief came yesterday," he began.

"Yes?" she prompted into the silence that he'd let develop.

"Oh, right. He said Candice's father wasn't dropping the charges and that the Department of Public Prosecutions had decided they had a good case and were going ahead. That means a proper trial and everything." The blockage that was stopping Sean talking seemed to have cleared and his words came out in a rush. "Even if I'm found not guilty it could take months and months and all the while I'll be stuck in here. I didn't mean to hurt anyone. I didn't know Candice was 15, she told me she was 16 and I believed her. It was only afterwards that I found out the truth, but by then it was too late. I'm not what that bastard officer calls me, nor those bullies. I'm not a paedophile, just a young man in love. You believe me, don't you miss?"

"You know I do, Sean."

"So last night, what with the visit from my brief and then a visit from the Whisperer, it was all just too much. I just couldn't keep going. I just, just," Sean faltered and then said softly, "I just wanted to die," the words pushed out of his mouth as though they were spoken on a dying breath.

They sat in silence for a moment, Emma allowing Sean to collect himself. Once he opened his eyes again she said, "Have I got this right? You said the Whisperer came again last night?"

"I think so, miss. Don't think I was dreaming. I just felt so alone, cut off from everyone, no one to turn to. And then he started on me. It was just too much."

Emma decided to deal with the information about the Whisperer later. For now she had to convince Sean to go on. Taking one of his hands in hers, she said, "Look, a listener is coming in again today, together with someone from the mental health team. Also Father Batty has been asking about you and would like to visit as well. Not only that but your mum will be in shortly. So, can you see how many people are concerned about you? You're not alone in all this, Sean, you have people you can lean on. So lean on them. We're all here to help you get through this."

She was rewarded with a watery smile.

"That's better," she said as she returned the smile.

"You mean you don't mind what I've done? What I'm in for? It doesn't make any difference to you?"

"It doesn't make any difference to any of us, Sean. We're not interested in what you've done in the past. We're only interested in how we can help you get through this experience. As for me, I'm interested in your welfare which also means I look at what you are keen on and what you are good at. If the worst did happen and you were convicted, I would talk to you about education, or vocational training. For however long or short a time you are with us, I want to make it as positive as possible. Let's view the time you have here as time to do something useful that we can capitalise on. There is another way, Sean, let us help you take that way."

"Th, th," was all Sean could manage. Emma continued to hold his hand as he cried, glad that now they seemed to be healing tears, rather than those born of despair.

On the way back to her office, she called in on Chief Robinson in his regimentally straight office and told him of the events of last night and asked him to thank the officers for their care and concern, which ultimately saved Sean Smith's life.

He regarded her for a moment. Then he said, "Thank you, Miss Harrison. Your recognition of the good work of my officers is appreciated. I hope you now understand that even though we can be tough on the lads, I wouldn't countenance any behaviour that was malicious or unfair."

"Speaking of that, Chief," Emma decided to take a leap in the dark. "It seemed there was an officer on the

Remand wing last night who was both malicious and unfair and it's not the first time it's happened."

At his questioning look she went on to tell him about her conversations with the lads and with the Governor about an officer everyone was calling the Whisperer. She also outlined the efforts she was taking to oust him.

"I was going to tell you all this, when I had more information, or evidence come to that. But, well, now seems as good a time as any."

"Yes, I see," Chief Robinson stood up from his chair and said, "Miss Harrison, honour has been my watchword for the past 20 odd years. It's what keeps my back straight and the backs of my officers. I won't let the honour of the prison be compromised. I'll support you in whatever course of action you think best and would like to thank you for the courtesy of letting me know what's going on. Without any anger or rancour, I might add," and for once a grin spread across his face.

"Thanks, Chief," Emma returned the smile and left for her office with a bit of a spring in her step from the Chief's praise. Praise was something everyone needed every now and again, she was beginning to realise.

Forty Four

That evening Emma was knee deep in papers. They were all over the carpet, the chairs and the dining table they never ate at. The papers were in piles, with notes on top. Notes that had names and dates on.

She'd just picked up a new sheet of paper when a voice said, "Hey," making her start. She'd been so engrossed in the documents she hadn't heard Billy's key in the door, nor it opening.

"Mmm," she said, her mouth full of a ball point pen. Laughing and taking it away, she called, "Hi, sorry I was engrossed in his lot."

Looking at her watch, she realised time had gotten away from her and it was already 9pm and there wasn't a meal even remotely made.

"I thought it might be something like that," he said.

"What?"

"I've been calling you."

Emma grabbed her phone and saw the missed calls and a couple of texts. "Oh, so sorry, love," she said and scrambling to her feet went over for a hug. "And I haven't even thought about anything to eat."

"It's alright I brought a take-away meal with me."

As she looked up at him, his eyes were smiling as well as his mouth. He really does understand, she realised. Understand that sometimes she could get carried away with her work, just as he did.

"Go and grab something to drink and I'll dish this lot up." Looking around he then said, "I think we'll eat in the kitchen, come on."

Once the drinks were poured, plates distributed and Chinese food served, Emma told Billy that eventually she'd managed to make some sense of the paperwork from the Accounts Department.

"And?"

"And there has regularly been the same supply officer, Dennis Budd, on three different wings, on the nights leading up to the three suicides."

Billy digested this information, then said, "I can tell from your face that there's more."

"Unfortunately, yes. Tom was on the same shifts. Surely Tom can't have anything to do with it, can he, Billy? I've worked with the bloke as a prison officer and I never saw him speak to anyone like that."

"But the evidence suggests that it is a possibility?"

Emma nodded her agreement. After skewering and eating a prawn she pointed her fork at Billy and said, "I did see him going into a cell and having a go at a kid the other day. Sean Smith, the one who is particularly vulnerable at the moment."

"What did the voice sound like on the phone? Did it sound like Tom?" Billy asked.

"I really couldn't say. It was a whisper and so flat and unemotional there was no cadence or ebb and flow as there is in a normal tone of voice. And it was on a mobile. Not the best instrument to try and identify a voice on and I was stood in the middle of a car park.

So, what do I do now?"

Billy thought for a moment. "You ring DI Briggs The bloke from Reading CID. You must tell him all about it and ask him to help."

"But won't it look strange calling in the Police? I don't want the Whisperer to think we're investigating him," Emma scrapped the last of a carton of curry onto her plate.

"No, I don't think so. The police have been in after every suicide, haven't they?"

"Yes, of course. That's normal procedure."

"Then it should be quite normal for you to contact Briggs about this and see if he can do anything. Even come into the prison. The police could just say they are there about another investigation or following up on an old one. What do you think?"

"I think I need to ring him first thing in the morning," she said and took a gulp of wine as if for Dutch courage.

Forty Five

"Emma, he's here."

"Thanks, Joan, send him in."

Emma took a deep breath as Sean Smith was led into her office. Crammed into the small space were also Father Batty and DI Briggs. The Chaplain looked serene, a state Emma had long strived for and never even come close to. Briggs looked as non-descript as ever, his saggy face and clothes in contrast to his sharp eyes. But during the race to find Leroy Carter, Emma had realised that Briggs was very good at his job and empathetic. Or at least as much as he could be, restricted as he was by the police policies and procedures. Emma had deliberately chosen the two men, trusting they would be kind enough, yet firm enough, to deal with Sean Smith. She could only hope they were doing the right thing by anticipating that Sean was strong enough to help with their planned sting operation.

As the lad sat down in the only free chair left, the accompanying officer looked at her. Emma inclined her head towards the door, indicating the officer could leave them alone. She didn't want anyone else being privy to their conversation. Equally, nor did she want the presence of an officer intimidating Sean. For that's why they were all there, to deal with the callous intimidation by a prison officer.

"Miss?" Sean said, looking around at the three of them.

"Sean, you know the Chaplain," Sean nodded, "and this is DI Briggs from Thames Valley Police."

"Hello, Sean," Briggs said.

"Why is he here? What have I done?" Sean ignored Briggs and looked at Emma.

"Nothing, Sean, it's just that we need your help," Emma said and went on to explain that they wanted to put in place a sting operation, to try and catch the Whisperer. The plan was to put cameras and microphones in Sean's cell and then make sure the two men they suspected were working on the wing that night, so the Whisperer could gain access to Sean. His last attempt at driving the boy to suicide had nearly worked, so they were sure he'd be wanting another go as soon as Sean was back on the wing from the hospital.

"You mean bug my cell?" Sean looked at Emma and then at the other two men. "I thought they were bugged already."

"No, that's an urban myth," Emma smiled, pushing her glasses back up her nose.

Father Batty said, "Sean, this man is not only making everyone feel bad, but he is committing a serious crime and has to be stopped. This is the only way we can think of to catch him."

Looking from one to the other once more, Sean said, "You mean this way I can take my revenge on him for what he's done to me?"

"If you want to look at it that way, then yes," replied Briggs. "But it will be the right kind of revenge. Outing him and stopping him harming any other vulnerable boys. And, of course, we will make him pay for the harm he's done."

"And I won't get into trouble?" Sean asked Emma.

"No," she said.

"What about the other officers? Won't they take it out on me? Punish me for helping you?"

"Not at all," said Father Batty, "because they won't know. This is a secret operation and the only ones who know about it are the Governor, Chief Robinson and us."

"And I guess it would look good on my record?" that question was fired at Briggs, making Emma smile. Sean may be vulnerable, but he wasn't stupid.

"Without a doubt, lad," he said.

At that Sean nodded his head and said the words Emma had been hoping to hear. "Alright, I'll do it. When do we start?"

Forty Six

Their first hurdle was to get Sean's cell wired up. He'd been moved back from the hospital wing into a single cell, rather than returning to his cell with Matt. Emma knew Sean wanted to be with his friend, but on balance they had decided that it wasn't wise to have another person privy to the operation. So Sean had agreed to be on his own. It was only for a little while and he felt he could cope with that.

A couple of nights after the initial meeting, Emma slipped into the back of the officer briefing at the start of the night shift. As Chief Robinson finished relaying the matters in hand to his officers he nodded at Emma and said, "Before we finished, Miss Harrison here wants a quick word."

"Thanks, Chief." Emma moved through the group to stand next to Chief Robinson. "It's just to let you know that I will be on the wing tonight, as will officers from Thames Valley Police."

A few eyebrows were raised at that piece of news.

"Anything to do with the suicides?" one asked.

"No, the police are here on an unrelated matter.

They want to interview Sean Smith about the physical attacks he has been suffering. As most of you know he's been attacked twice now by a group of bullies. But as he is so vulnerable both mentally and physically, it was felt it would be better to have him interviewed in his cell, at night, after lock up. That way none of the inmates will know the police have ever been here and Sean will feel safe talking about the attacks and giving descriptions of the bullies to the police. It's important that this interview is conducted surreptitiously. It's taken us a long time to persuade him to help. Please respect our need for secrecy."

"It's all a bit strange, though," called an officer.

"Yes, it's never been done before," said another.

"So why can't it be done now?" challenged Emma. "The Governor and the police have decided that this is the best way of handling it from an inmate welfare point of view. I'm in total agreement. And as I'm in charge of inmate welfare I've given the go ahead. Thank you, Chief," and Emma walked out of the meeting, back straight, head up, hoping to God it would work.

They had chosen a night when neither Tom, nor Dennis Budd were on duty. They were both due back tomorrow night, which should give the police plenty of time to put the bugs in place and check the equipment was working properly.

"Alright, Sean?" Emma asked, as the visiting party arrived at his cell. They'd decided to come after the 8pm lock up but before lights out. 10pm was chosen as by then most of the lads had settled down and were watching the television. All around the wing could be heard various programmes. Some goggle boxes were showing the same channel, but there were slight time lags in the sound. Others emitted a discordant soundtrack from an entirely different programme.

At their arrival in his cell, Sean huddled into the far corner of his bed.

"I'll just stay here, out of the way," he said.

"There's nothing to worry about," said Briggs. "We'll be in and out in no time. What we're looking for are a couple of places to point cameras at the inspection hatch. We also need a microphone on the back of the door, or just above on the lintel to catch the whispers."

Emma sat down on the bed, to keep out of the way while Briggs and his colleague scanned the space, but also to keep Sean company. The work didn't take long. There weren't many options in a small prison cell, a prison cell that was now severely over-crowded.

"The trick is not to look at the cameras," said Briggs.

"I won't because I won't know where they are," mumbled Sean who had pulled his legs up, had his head on them, and his arms around his head.

Emma hoped to goodness he was alright and could handle this. By the look of him Briggs was wondering the same, but he soon turned his attention back to the policeman he'd brought with him.

"Do you need to plug them in or anything? I don't know much about this sort of equipment," Emma admitted.

"No, no need for anything like that. They are battery powered and connected via wireless to the main CCTV system. Also they're voice activated, so nothing will happen until someone speaks. That way, Sean doesn't need to worry about being watched all the time. Alright, Sean?"

That piece of information seemed to get through to the lad and he lifted his head slightly and nodded, reminding Emma of a timid tortoise gingerly poking his head out from under his shell.

"That's not so bad then, thanks," he said.

"There'll be a dedicated CCTV camera trained on your cell door the whole time. Oh, and we'd prefer it if you keep the light on as long as you can."

"Until lights out, you mean?"

"Yes. Just keep your lights on and they'll go off automatically at 2am," Emma reminded Sean.

"Okay, miss."

As Briggs and his colleague finished and packed up their stuff, Emma turned to Sean. "We won't be watching or listening tonight, Sean, so don't worry about that. We'll just be checking the equipment, then leaving. And as far as we're aware the Whisperer isn't on duty tonight, so you're safe from him. Are you alright?"

"Yes, miss." But Sean's face looked drawn and Emma hoped the tension wouldn't do any harm to his fragile mental health. She'd hate for anything to damage the progress he'd made.

"You're very brave to do this, Sean," she said. "We can't thank you enough. Oh, by the way, Father Batty will be along in the morning. So until then try and sleep, eh?"

"Yes, miss. But I'll leave the TV on if that's okay."

"Of course. But Sean, we need you to turn off the TV by about 10pm tomorrow night. We want the officer to think you've gone to sleep early, so as to give him plenty of opportunity to come around and start to wind you up. Perhaps you could read?"

Sean looked puzzled then his face cleared. "I've got that book you lent me, miss, that sci-fi one. I'll start on that."

"Well, if you pull this off tomorrow, I'll buy you the

whole series as a present."

"You're on, Miss," Sean grinned and Emma left his cell to join the two policemen, feeling more confident about this whole venture than she had done earlier in the day. Sean was making an enormous effort to help them and had put his faith in her. She only hoped she could live up to that sort of pressure and that she was correct in her guess that the Whisperer was either Tom Collins or Dennis Budd. Only time would tell.

Forty Seven

Emma had trouble concentrating following day. She looked at her watch at least every half an hour, which made the time drag even more. She couldn't settle to anything and ended up chatting on the phone to Billy a few times, until he told her, good naturedly, to piss off so he could get some work done.

She didn't go near Sean that day, but knew that his listener was with him, Father Batty had seen him and Sean had a scheduled visit from his mum. They'd also allowed him a phone call to his girlfriend, Candice. It wouldn't normally have been allowed, letting him speak to his victim, but well, he needed a show of faith from them and as the pair were desperate to communicate, Emma and the Governor had agreed to Sean's request. They hoped that would give him the boost he needed. His mum had told them that Candice was just as desperate to talk to Sean, as he was to talk to her. But Emma took the precaution of speaking to Candice herself first, before she allowed Sean to make the call. To her intense relief Candice was in tears when told she could speak to Sean on the phone that day. In between sobs that she tried to gulp back, she told Emma how much she loved Sean and wanted him to know that she promised to wait for him, no matter what happened.

Emma kept brooding on what might go wrong. Perhaps Tom wouldn't turn up for work? Or Budd? She wasn't sure that Sean was strong enough to try again if either one of them didn't show. Or what if neither were the Whisperer? Or what if the Whisperer was on the wing but decided not to do anything, because there'd been a leak and he'd found out Sean and his cell were under surveillance?

None of these thoughts were conducive to work, or to her keeping her nerve, so in the end she decided to go out for a walk at the end of the day. Somehow being outside, around people, breathing in fresh air helped and she mooched around the shops, window shopping for a while until it was time to go back. It was a good job she didn't smoke, she decided, for God knows what her cigarette consumption would have been that day.

It was still only 8pm when she joined Chief Robinson in the main control room and they checked they had sound and vision from Sean's cell. Lock-up was just starting and they clearly saw and heard an officer speak to Sean, then close and lock his door. A little while later Briggs arrived and the three of them settled down to wait. The control room was normally manned by four officers, one for each wing in the prison and they'd looked up enquiringly as first the Chief, then Emma and finally Briggs arrived. Once they were all there, Chief Robinson had a quiet word and told the officers what was going on. From that moment on, they were not allowed to leave the room under any circumstances. Chief Robinson told them if they wanted the loo, to tie a knot in it and wait until the operation was over. He also warned against anyone of them attempting to communicate what was happening with the wing under surveillance. Any abnormal messages that were intended to hamper the operation would be met with instant dismissal. No exceptions. By the end of the little pep talk, the four were sweating with tension and it hadn't helped Emma's nerves any.

It wasn't long before it was time for an officer to do the rounds on Sean's landing. The task fell to Tom. Emma watched him as he walked along the landings, striding from camera to camera, stopping occasionally. Opening the hatch on some of the cells, but not others. As he approached Sean's door Emma rubbed the palms of her hands on her trousers to try and dry them. She put a finger up to her mouth and began to chew on the nail. A few more steps and he would be there. Three more. Two more. Tom stopped. Not outside Sean's door, but close by. He was completely still apart from his hands, which were clenching and unclenching, as though the gesture was an external sign of an inner turmoil. Emma held her breath, as did the others in the room. No one dared speak. All were glued to the screen. It seemed that Tom was itching to do something. He strained towards Sean's door. Took the last step... then continued walking along the landing.

They all exhaled a collective sigh.

"Bloody hell," said Briggs. "That was a close one, I was sure he was going to do something."

"So was I," said Emma. "I was so afraid just then that Tom was our Whisperer, but it looks like he isn't."

"Only looks like, Miss Harrison," Chief Robinson said. "We've a long night ahead of us yet."

Forty Eight

Sean had turned off his television as requested and pulled Emma's book towards him. She had asked that he turn his television off, so they could better record the officer's voice as he whispered his vitriolic diatribe through the open hatchway. No one wanted any background noise competing with the whispers. For prosecution purposes the audio recording had to be as clear as possible. Sean was trying his best to read, but was finding it hard to escape into the fictional world. Books had always been his love and he knew that they could be a way back for him. A way back from this awful depression that was at last beginning to lift. Being able to do something positive to stop anyone else being psychologically damaged had spurred him on and was the reason he'd agreed to help.

Just then Sean heard footsteps approach his cell. Straining to hear, he held his breath, wondering if the heavy breathing he could hear was his, or from someone outside his door. He didn't think he'd ever been so bloody frightened in all his life. But why was that? Rationally, Sean knew he was safe in his cell. He knew the officer they called the Whisperer, whoever it was, wouldn't come in, just talk through the hatch. It just showed how psychologically vulnerable he'd become, to be afraid of a few words. The children's rhyme of 'sticks and stones may break my bones, but words will never hurt me', flitted through his mind. What a load of bollocks that was.

All was quiet once again outside his cell, so he relaxed a little, placed his book open on his chest, leaned back and thought of Candice. What a difference that had made to him, being able to talk to her on the phone. To know that she still loved him. He remembered the feel of her lips on his when they first kissed, a light caress that had held so much promise. He knew they were still very young, but for many people young love had stood the test of time. He hoped theirs would too.

And then he heard it. The squeaking of shoes coming along the landing. All the air seemed to be sucked out of the cell and he began to feel as though he were suffocating. The walls closed in and he was vaguely aware he was starting to panic, from claustrophobia and fear. He felt the air being forced out of his lungs as his chest became gripped in a vice-like embrace. He remembered what Matt had told him. When a panic attack strikes, he had to try and regulate his breathing. Breathe in, two thousand. Out, two thousand. In, two thousand. Out, two thousand. That helped. Although it didn't take away the sound of the rubber soled shoes that he could still hear walking up the landing. Getting closer and closer. Sean decided to try the trick Father Batty had taught him. Think good thoughts. The best thing in his life was Candice. So he said her name over and over again in his head, so that when the whispering started, he wouldn't hear it.

Forty Nine

"Miss Harrison," one of the officer's in the control room called. "Someone's walking along Sean's landing."

Emma moved over to the monitor and followed the officer's progress, but could only see his back. All officers being dressed in the same uniform, it was hard to determine who the officer was. The only clue was the hair. Short and brown. That could describe one of several officers. There was no other clue to aid identification.

DI Briggs fiddled with some buttons on the console and suddenly the squeak of rubber soled shoes filled the control room. The sound picked up by the microphones placed at Sean's door. They'd decided to install two. One inside and one outside, just to make sure.

Emma, Briggs and Chief Robinson watched the monitors as avidly as picture goers so invested in a film they saw or heard nothing else. Oblivious to her surroundings, Emma watched as the officer stepped closer to Sean's cell door. The man took a surreptitious look around to see if he anyone was watching. As he turned his head to look behind him, they got a good look at his face.

Opening the hatch that creaked like something out of a gothic horror movie, the officer placed his lips close to the side of the hatch.

"I see you, Sean. You can't hide from me."

Flicking her vision to the monitor showing the inside of Sean's cell, she could see the boy was sitting on his bunk, knees up, with his hands over his ears. His lips were moving soundlessly.

"Covering your ears won't help. It won't take away the filthy, disgusting thoughts that you have. You can't change the fact that you're a bastard. That you have a dark mass of evil inside you. The flaw you have in your character that makes you desire children."

Tears were running down Sean's cheeks. He was shaking his head violently from side to side.

"I've told you before. I know you for what you are," the taunting continued. "A perverted nonce, not fit to walk the streets, not fit to be alive. It's about time you did us all a favour and bowed out. Your mum would be better off without you. Without a piece of trash like you. You're not fit to be called her son."

By now Sean was tearing at his hair. Grabbing handfuls of it and pulling hard, the noise of him sobbing filling the small cell. Emma was seriously worried about him and was poised to leave the control room and run to his cell, but Chief Robinson must have seen her reaction and placing a hand on her arm shook his head.

Seemingly satisfied at last, the Whisperer fell silent, closed the hatch and continued on his way.

"Is that good enough for you?" Chief Robinson asked Briggs.

"Perfect, thanks, we've got audio and video footage of him. Well done everyone."

"It's not us that did it, it was Sean," Emma reminded them. "I just hope it the ordeal hasn't done too much damage. Anyway, isn't it time we picked the Whisperer up. Arrested him. Got him off the wing."

"Now, Miss Harrison, a little more patience is needed I'm afraid. We're not going to him. I'm going to get him to come to us," said Chief Robinson.

"But he might get away!"

"You seem to have forgotten that we're in a prison," a smile cracked his normally curmudgeonly face. "He can't get away and I certainly don't want to cause a scene on the wing. Alright?"

"Yes, Chief," replied Emma, her face burning with embarrassment.

Chief Robinson spoke into his microphone and so began the most agonising five minutes of Emma' life. She fiddled. She faddled. She started conversations she was unable to finish. She wished she could ring Billy. She wished she could go to Sean. She chewed at a nail. Until a last there was a knock at the door.

And Dennis Budd walked into the Control Room.

Fifty

It was with more than a little satisfaction that Emma walked into Governor Sharpe's office first thing the next morning, to report on the successful operation last night.

In conclusion she said, "Dennis Budd was arrested and taken straight to Reading Police Station last night. I'm just off to see Sean Smith now. Geoff Fox and I were with him last night, to reassure him that the ordeal was over. He needed to know that the officer had been arrested by the police and would no longer be able to enter Reading Prison. He was taken to the hospital wing last night, just as a precaution."

"Is he going to sign a statement?"

"Absolutely, Governor. DI Briggs is coming in later today to take his statement, while he is in the hospital, so there is little or no chance of any reprisals against Sean. The less people know about this whole operation, the better."

"Indeed. But I'm going to have to order an enquiry. Questions will be asked," he blustered. No doubt because he had to make sure he covered his arse, as usual, Emma thought.

"Certainly, sir, I'm sure all questions will be answered and loop holes closed," Emma soothed. On the one hand she hated herself for being placatory, but on the other congratulated herself on not getting upset and taking his comments as a personal slight, when they probably weren't meant that way.

Afterwards sitting at her desk with her first coffee of the day, she thought back to her conversation with Billy last night. She was still on a high when she'd arrived home and was so glad to see him still awake. If he hadn't been she would have woken him up. They sat in bed, discussing the operation over cups of hot chocolate and she told him that she hoped some good would come out of it all. It seemed to have highlighted the vulnerable state of some of the lads that came into the establishment.

"I know I can't save every boy that comes into Reading, but as you said before, at least I can help some of them and that even small victories are worthwhile."

"Well I don't think that you can count this as a small victory," Billy smiled, leaning over and kissing her, "I think it's a bloody big one. Not only have you helped Sean but I rather think you've learned to help yourself."

"You mean I'm more diplomatic that I used to be?"

"Well, maybe just a bit," he teased and ducked out of the way as she swung a pillow at his head.

Fifty One

The Whisperer sat opposite DI Briggs in an interview room in Reading Police Station, composed and silent. He had refused to answer any of Brigg's questions. In fact so far he had said absolutely nothing at all. No matter how hard Briggs pressed him for information on the lads that he had been whispering to, or wanted to know why he had taunted them, he refused to speak.

At one point Briggs leaned over the desk and told Budd he was going to prison for a very long time indeed. As though the thought of going to prison was intimidating. At that, Budd couldn't resist a wry smile. For what none of the policemen seemed to understand was that, for him, being incarcerated was not a threat. Prison was where he felt most useful, most needed. It was exactly where he loved to be. Amongst the flotsam and jetsam of human life. Where he could practice his art.

His eyes lit up at the thought of being surrounded by all those useless, worthless individuals who didn't deserve to be alive. The hated nonces. The murderers. Armed robbers. Gangland members. People who selfishly took what they wanted, without a thought for their victims. But more importantly, with no thought for their own families. For the agonies that their wives, children and mothers were subjected to, because of their crimes. As a result of the incarceration of their loved ones.

Oh yes, he would have lots of subjects to practice his dark art on to his heart's content. He would miss his diary, of course, which detailed his successes since he first began whispering the stark truths to his victims. He didn't think the police would find it. It was well hidden. And anyway, he could always start a new one. He could work out a code to write it in, so that no one would be able to read the true meaning behind his words.

When DI Briggs left the room, shaking his head in frustration because of his inability to get Budd to talk, the Whisperer allowed wide toothy grin to light up his toady face.

Meet the Author

I do hope you've enjoyed Mortal Judgment. If so, perhaps you would be kind enough to post a review on Amazon. Reviews really do make all the difference to authors and it is great to get feedback from you, the reader.

If you haven't read one of my novels before, you may be interested in the Sgt Major Crane books, following Tom Crane and DI Anderson as they take on the worst crimes committed in and around Aldershot Garrison. At the time of writing there are seven Sgt Major Crane crime thrillers. In order, they are: Steps to Heaven, 40 Days 40 Nights, Honour Bound, Cordon of Lies, Regenerate, Hijack and Glass Cutter. All books are available from Amazon:

You can keep in touch through my website where you can sign up to join my mailing list and in return get a free ebook! Everyone who signs up gets a free copy of Steps to Heaven (kindle or pdf). I'm also on Twitter @wendycartmell and can be contacted directly by email at: w_cartmell@hotmail.com

Happy reading until the next time...

Printed in Great Britain
by Amazon